sol.

INTERNATIONAL Date LINE

Dawn Howat

INTERNATIONAL Date LINE

GREAT PLAINS
PUBLICATIONS

Great Plains Publications
420 – 70 Arthur Street
Winnipeg, MB R3B 1G7
www.greatplains.mb.ca

Great Plains Publications gratefully acknowledges the financial support provided for its publishing program by the Government of Canada through the Book Publishing Industry Development Program (BPIDP); the Canada Council for the Arts; the Manitoba Department of Culture, Heritage and Tourism; and the Manitoba Arts Council.

Design & Typography by Gallant Design Ltd.
Printed in Canada by Friesens

CANADIAN CATALOGUING IN PUBLICATION DATA

Main entry under title:
Howat, Dawn
  International date line / Dawn Howat.

ISBN 1-894283-38-4

I.   Title
PS8565.O8435I57   2003   C813'.6   C2003-910138-X
PR9199.4.H68I57   2003

To My Parents

PROLOGUE

The Dog Howls

This would *so* never happen in Canada.

And even as I think this, I am aware that it is the thought of a boorish North American tourist and that I ought to be ashamed of myself. But then standing here in a hateful and unprecedented nic fit, about the twentieth person in line at the laughably-stocked grocery store on the corner of Rakoczi and Szentkiralyi in downtown Budapest, I can't help but be furious. Or at the very least extremely irritated.

This grocery store sucks.

To my left, the stock boy is ogling me. Without the slightest pretense of nonchalance, I might add. From behind him comes the haughty glare of the security guard, the one who seems to constantly patrol the same box of flaccid vegetables and whose wages might—present situation taken into account—be better served by an additional checkout lady.

Hungarian service does not exist, I think, quite lucidly. In fact I would bet there isn't even an equivalent word for service in all of the impossibility of the Hungarian language. And not only that there is no equivalent word for it, but that the concept itself is about as relevant as an aeroplane at a bus stop...about as relevant as a Canadian at an identity hearing...about as relevant as...

Please note: The use of both British and American spelling standards throughout this work is intentional.

All I want is to buy a pack of cigarettes. But I want this very badly. And I want it now. Because quitting smoking is frankly not all it's cracked up to be. It's true that I could go instead to the cigarette shop down the street, but there lurks the indignity of trying to communicate a specific brand, with all of the attendant options that that entails—light, ultra light, extra light, King Size, regular size, 100's—and I fear that my wretched, nicotine-deprived brain is just not up to such subtleties of communication. Plus I speak no Hungarian. So I remain here in this supermarket of apathy where I can simply choose the brand I want from the shelf by the cash desk, which is still twenty people away, just by the way.

There seems to be some sort of hold-up at the register. I see glazed eyes scanning, sense the still limbo of a price-check in progress. A checkout woman who is clearly on her break ambles up to the front of the line and butts in to buy her own pack of cigarettes. It's outrageous that this would happen, could happen, is happening.

The line waits silently. The line waits calmly. The line barely breathes.

There is no other line.

This would *so* never happen in Canada, I think. Again.

I notice that I am trembling—jittery hands, twitchy face. Standard withdrawal symptoms obviously. But no, it was that dog. I can't shake the sound of that goddamn dog.

It was running full-tilt down the sidewalk. No leash. No owner. I don't care who you are: you *will* be disturbed by a flat-eyed husky charging towards you on an impossibly narrow Budapestian sidewalk. (Especially if, like me, your whole being is focussed on reacquiring a nicotine habit which was so very recently and so very foolishly abandoned.)

Rabid, you think immediately.

Holy crap, you think immediately.

This is the end, you think immediately.

Or at least I did, holding my breath and perhaps even closing my eyes a little until the husky went sprinting past me, as little concerned with me it turned out as its owner was with it. I saw a potential owner finally: a squat woman with a dirty t-shirt and untethered breasts, rounding a corner some fifty feet behind her uncontrollable and potentially rabid and probably lethal dog.

A plastic shopping basket presses impatiently against my back. *Goddamnit.* I twist my throbbing head around to glare at what turns out to be a hunched old woman with geometric cheekbones. That dog on the loose was an accident waiting to happen, I think, glaring and exasperated and irrational. Not that I wanted the damn thing to get hit, but still. I turn away from the severely cheekboned woman and stare at the stalled line ahead. By the time I get up there it will be hour seventy of this withdrawal and then is it even worth it? Shouldn't I just continue *not* smoking, close as I am to the seventy-two-hour mark, the beginning of the end of this crippling withdrawal, the beginning of the end of this unseemly chemical torture?

The dog howled like a betrayed child.

It was struck down in the middle of the street. I heard the thud—substantial. And then the howl—childlike. But I didn't see any of it happen; the whole thing took place just behind me. The sauntering woman whom I had almost passed, and who indeed seemed to be the owner of the dog, rushed past me then, her untethered breasts swinging unselfconsciously in rhythm with her shocked and hanging jaw.

I turned around. I saw that other people on the street were stopped as well, frozen just like me, unsure whether to feign indifference or burst into tears. My skin was covered in goose bumps. I could hear the dog howling, howling, howling, in a voice that could be anyone's—even mine—but I could not actually see it. There were parked cars in the way.

...about as relevant as white cotton underpants on display at the grocery store.

Though it turns out that this actually is relevant, as there is a wire bin brimming with panties not five feet away. I will never understand this culture, I think. This is an indecipherable culture.

The dog continued to howl.

Are you sure you want to see, I asked myself even as I stepped out onto the street for a better view. Despite my shock I was careful to avoid the plentiful piles of dog shit scattered across the pavement.

That sound, that awful fucking *howl*, enhanced by a visual: the husky lying on its side, struck down in the very middle of the road, the woman kneeling beside it. I was thankful there was no ghastly blood or gore to endure, yet it seemed impossible for blood and guts *not* to accompany such a penetrating sound.

People drive too quickly here, I think, still gazing at the bin of underpants. Two pairs for seven hundred *forints*. What is that, two dollars per panty? Not bad...not bad at all...

Still the dog howled.

Farther away were two stopped vehicles: a truck in front of a small car. The driver of the truck was out of his vehicle, the door hanging wide open. He was yelling at the occupants of the small car. It was unclear which of these two vehicles had actually hit the dog. It is still unclear.

More people with hands over their mouths arrived on the street to stare at the howling husky. It was trying to lick one of its legs, even as it yowled.

I thought: Shouldn't I do something?

The woman picked the dog up. The howling stopped— sudden, like the relief of that first drag. Absurdly, she cradled the husky like a child in her arms—its weight had to be considerable—and trotted back in her original direction, but on the opposite side of the street this time.

An older woman followed her, said something, was ignored.

Do I *need* more underpants?

The truck, and then the car, drove off.

When the woman reached the supermarket corner, she set the husky down on the ground again. It instantly resumed its cry.

I close my eyes.

That sound. *That awful fucking sound.*

I break suddenly from the haphazard line and make for the supermarket exit. I can feel the security guard eyeing me suspiciously. As if anyone could be blamed for stealing flaccid vegetables or Hungarian paprika or even underpants instead of waiting on this non-existent, not to mention untranslatable service.

Weaving recklessly through the crowd, I slam my way out the door and veer towards the cigarette shop. I will act out smoking and take whatever they hand me, I do not care, for frankly I just need a cancer stick, any kind of inevitably lethal cancer stick. It's been sixty-nine hours— *sixty-nine hours!* And now I've given up on giving up, but somehow I'm unable to accomplish even this. *I cannot seem to quit quitting!?*

I ignore the person on the street whom I have almost knocked over, am sick of being the nice one, the *accommodating* one, the one who always gets out of *everyone else's* way. Get out of *my* way, buster. Today you'll get the hell out of my way!

But it would seem, on this most unfortunate of afternoons, that I cannot successfully achieve even this. For before I can take another step the person I have almost trampled speaks to me.

"Anna?" the person says, and I turn around with my angry mouth open, ready to blast off like I've never blasted off before until I realize that not only has this person spoken to me in English—which is a shock considering that I am smack-dab in the center of Budapest, Hungary—but also that he has said my name.

I look at this person, my head cocked. "Uh…?"

"Ian," he says, pointing at his devilishly skinny chest, which I have to admit looks smooth and enticing even from underneath a loose Diesel t-shirt. "Old Man's Pub."

The fucking TESL wanker!

"I-an," I repeat. (Did I even know that this was his name?)

He grins at me. "How *are* you?"

I smile sheepishly back at him.

Somehow we are shaking hands—shaking, shaking, shaking. I glance at the grocery store just behind Ian's right shoulder. A whimper courses through me as I attempt to form a coherent sentence. Finally I say: "To tell you the truth, I'm fucking dying for a cigarette."

But I can hardly even hear my own voice, never mind register Ian's reaction, for that howling husky is still running laps inside my skull.

Hoooooooooow-weeeeeeeeeel, the dog cries.

And I know it's irrational, I know it cannot be, but still I get the feeling, the almost incontrovertible feeling that that husky was trying to tell me something. Crazy I know, but it suddenly occurs to me that that goddamn dog was howling at *me…*

PART ONE

Before The Dog

He must have been obsessing over *Fight Club* again.

The buzz said: You are not your possessions.

The buzz said: Fling off your media-manipulated façade.

The buzz said: Be real.

But the crazy part is that Jack and I (mostly Jack) actually listened.

I can't get that movie out of my head, He e-mailed me from Seattle. *We totally have to do that.*

What? Like beat people up?

No, no. The other stuff. The quit-your-crap-life, abandon-your-complacency stuff.

But I didn't know what the hell He was talking about. I sure as hell never thought He meant I should quit my job, sell my Toronto condo, farm out my cat's special brand of affection and fly to Eastern—or is it Central now?—Europe so that He could stand me up in an internet café aptly christened Budapest Bytes. Not even in my wildest dreams did I imagine that that was what the American bastard could mean.

Still I sold, discarded, and gave away all of my possessions, not to mention the Dubble Bubble cat—so named for the pink hue of her nose—which may be the worst thing I have ever done in this lifetime, though god knows there seems to be ample room here for improvement, and bought a one-way ticket to Budapest, thereby severing myself from virtually everything and everyone that I know, not to mention all access to the popular media or at least media I can understand, i.e. English media, so that I might attempt this business of being real. And more importantly embark upon a European love-fest with Jack, perhaps the most important man of my past.

I thought: Surely my impeccable taste will prevail despite living in a media vacuum. (This was in Toronto.)

I thought: Surely I will still be a sought-after member of the international style council. (Again, back in Toronto.)

I thought: Surely I'll be able to locate a decent hair salon. (Toronto.)

Though I confess, now, lately, at times, I may be just slightly afraid for my chances...

I am twenty-nine.

My name is Anna Woods, and I am sitting in a singularly dreary hotel/apartment room in Budapest, Hungary. Or rather I am lying in one. Quite foolishly really, I am waiting for the above-mentioned Jack to join me here, which still may or may not actually happen. Because my options are to wait here for Him to eventually show or to go home empty-handed, to go home *sans* love story, or in fact any story at all. And frankly, I'm not sure my already sickly romantic reputation could withstand the blow.

I am also, in some sort of pathetic last-ditch effort to grow up and be responsible before I'm thirty—and also because Jack just e-mailed me to tell me what a snap it was—I am also attempting to give up the nicotine. Again. But unlike other attempts, which were wholly unpleasant yet somehow manageable, this attempt has rendered me quite paralyzed. I find that I am now unable to leave this room. Or even, for that matter, this sweaty, pull-out, single-sized chair-bed.

Incapable.

At present.

So I lie here in a contemptible sweat and try to reconstruct the beginning of this misstep, the start of this (now) obvious mistake. And at first I thought it must be my friends who were to blame. After all, shouldn't they have said something to deter me from this obviously ill-fated mission? But then I realize it goes back further than that. It goes back to Jack, the Jack who is still—in case I haven't already mentioned it—back in Seattle.

Clearly this is Jack's fault.

Did you see that goddamn movie? He wrote. *Did you see that?*

I did, but I sure as hell never thought it would come to this.

Much to my stood-up chagrin, I have discovered that Budapest is a very romantic city. Everywhere you look there are couples. I could be one of those couples, I think, I thought, remembering them as I lie here immobilized by an unprecedented wretchedness due to depreciating nicotine levels in my bloodstream. Why can't I be one of those couples?

But I suppose it's a rhetorical question, considering that I already know the answer, considering how obvious the answer really is: Because Jack is still back in Seattle.

Jack wrote: *Don't go anywhere.*

Jack wrote: *I've had an unexpected, unavoidable delay.*

Jack wrote: *But I'll be there June 22nd.*

Which is just so clearly polite-speak for: *I'm standing you up.* And that was on May 19th, more than four weeks ago. Jack has kept me waiting here for more than a month. And so what choice did I have but to discover Budapest? What choice but to play the solitary, eager tourist, to play with the likes of the Londoner and the Frenchman and—

Lord love us, I want a cigarette. It's difficult for me to focus on anything beyond my desire for a cigarette...

Perhaps I should mention my terrible apprehension.

Directly above my prone body hovers a jagged crack in the ceiling. And perhaps due to the glaring absence of a TV, I am quite transfixed by this crack. The ceiling is double-arched and reminds me of the McDonald's logo, or even a brassiere awaiting a giant pair of breasts, though I'm not sure which of these two icons I would rather it resembled, i.e. which of these two icons is the least psychologically damning. The ominous crack runs alongside a too-thin support beam which forms the imaginary breastbone, or if you prefer, the middle dip of the *M*. I am convinced, have been convinced for days (or at least a few hours), that it is only a matter of time before that crack gives way. Before the beam snaps. Before my double-arched ceiling comes crashing down on both me and my misery.

And it was recently, only in the wee hours of this morning in fact, while staring up at this foreboding rift that I came to the upsetting, yet not entirely shocking realization that I am an idiot, that this being an idiot is the real me: the possession-less, media-free, being-real me. For who else but a complete idiot would wait for four weeks in a foreign country for some unreliable (I see that now) American asshole named Jack?

Such revelations could probably be avoided if only I had a room with a television.

I really really really want a cigarette. Really really really...

Still, I suppose it must also be said (though not to Jack) that this last month has not been a total idiotic disaster either. Living off of the proceeds of a recently abandoned life can be quite exhilarating. Especially since Budapest, as it turns out, is jam-packed with spectacle.

I've seen Fisherman's Bastion and the Castle District. I've climbed Citadella Hill. I've spent a full day in the healing waters of the Gellert thermal baths—though it occurs to me now that an additional session or two mightn't be a bad idea. I've jogged, or maybe more precisely, jog-walked around Margrit Island. I've sipped coffee on Andrassy. I've lounged in City Park where I saw a young man with a disturbing resemblance to Jack. (Or at least a resemblance to how Jack used to look, since I have no current reference for comparison. The young man was playing hackeysack with his girlfriend. He took his shirt off. He was twenty-two, tops. I watched them (him) all afternoon. I willed him to look at me—not in a desperate kind of pathetic way, just casual-like. But he did not. He stared at the hackeysack, and at his girlfriend with whom he seemed quite smitten, and neither of them glanced at me all afternoon. Nor even in my general direction, though I cunningly changed my position several times.) I've wandered through Westend Mall and around, but not through, the gigantic, under-construction Parliament. I've visited the faded Communist splendor of Statue Park, taken a city bus tour, floated on a Danube boat tour, strolled Vaci utca and Vorosmarty ter, roared at the lions of Chain Bridge, pastried at Café Gerbaud, tormented a Londoner, fucked a Frenchman.

Well, you get the idea. You can see I haven't been paralyzed by idiocy the *entire* time I've been here. You can see that at some point I acted at least slightly normal.

Cigarette, cigarette, cigarette...

I've been mulling over my last entry and I fear that the quick (unintended) mention(s) I made of both the Londoner and the Frenchman may reflect poorly on me, perhaps should not have been mentioned at all. And therefore I feel

----

I ought to take a moment to explain, perhaps even to defend my actions.

Allow me just a moment to explain.

The Frenchman wouldn't tell me his name.

It was four-thirty in the morning. The lights were on inside the bar—Old Man's Pub. Ignoring the burly Hungarian bouncers, we were slouched by the exit, finishing this Frenchman's beer in a leisurely and dignified and frankly continental manner.

I was one hundred per cent filled with lager and delight.

We'd met maybe four hours ago. At this point I knew he was French, I knew he was an insurance broker, I knew he was perhaps not the most skilled of dancers, but I hadn't yet inquired as to his name. (Because this is not always requisite information for me, all right?) And I might never have noticed this omission, but for the fact that he brought it up.

"I love that you have not asked me my name," he smirked.

"Oh my god," I laughed. "What's your name?"

He winked a single wide brown French eye. "Now you must wait. There is a French proverb. *Dans la maison du bonheur, la salle d'attente est la plus grande.*"

I tried to decipher it using my mandatory grade-school French. "In the house of...say it again."

"*Dans la maison du bonheur, la salle d'attente est la plus grande.* It does not translate that well," he said in the enchanting accent which would soon tickle my ear with dirty foreign words. (It's a very sexy language, this French French. Not Quebec French obviously, which is a whole other kettle of *poisson*.)

I said: "*Dans la maison du* what?"

"Ooh," he cringed. "Your accent. It is so harsh."

(You see?)

I shrugged.

He said: "In the house of good times, the waiting room is the biggest room."

I had smiled sadly, distantly. Somehow Jack came to mind. Jack is the biggest room, I'd instantly thought, despite the nameless international summit I was then holding. Despite the fact that Jack, due to arrive in Budapest that very afternoon (May 19th to be exact) had in fact just stood me up (this was over four weeks ago), which led to an afternoon of Hungarian pints on a patio near my apartment/hotel where I bumped into a bawdy Scottish woman and a mumbling Irishman who talked me into an unnecessary series of shots of the local absinthe (inexplicably entitled Unicum) in this very bar and subsequently, to this very Frenchman.

Perhaps *Monsieur* could feel me slipping away.

"Who cuts your hair?" the Frenchman gruffly demanded.

"What?"

"Your hair, it is perfect for your face. *Parfait!*"

I'd smiled. I'd forgotten all about his name. I'd decided right then and there to fuck that asshole Jack by fucking this Frenchman, this *Monsieur Parfait*.

Because I'd just been stood up.

Because I was filled with lager and Unicum and delight.

Because the Frenchman reached out his hand to touch my golden locks and once again exclaim: "*Parfait!*" (It goes without saying that this was several weeks ago.)

And then *Monsieur Parfait* artfully polished off his beer and accompanied me back to my singularly dreary hotel/apartment room, which was conveniently located only a few blocks away and where I learned many things about him, but not, as it were, his name.

But still I thought: Take that, Jack. Take that.

Although the entire experience was a (hazy) delight, the thing that perhaps pleased me most about the unexpected French *amour* was that it gave me an amusing (I think) line to e-mail back to all of my friends, a line which I also hoped might help to put my questionable romantic reputation back on track.

Met a Frenchman who literally charmed the pants right off of me, I wrote repeatedly, but separately to each of my e-mail pals, none of whom I specifically missed yet, though I hoped to soon. *It took me four days before I even realized what happened. That's how fucking charming the French are, you don't even know they're doing it!*

"Are all Canadian women like you?" he had said the next morning, still gazing reverently at my hair. "I think I must move to Canada *immediatement.*"

Although in retrospect, lying here staring at the double concavity of the ceiling in my room, quite paralyzed and sweaty as I am, in retrospect these *communiques* do smack more of desperate boasting than wit, don't they?

But again, if Jack had not stood me up that day I would never have drunk all that cheap draught, never mind anything named Unicum, never mind—*fucking Jack!*

Does this make me look any better? I'm unsure whether the explanation helps or hinders. I am hardly, truth be told, able to think at all, considering that I am on the crucial (or so I like to think) thirteenth hour of my nicotine withdrawal.

It is 7 a.m.

It is June 18th.

It is Monday.

My chest is making funny shapes. The left side twitches at an opposing rhythm to the right.

Left.

Right.

Left, left.

Right.

Both sides spasm forcefully enough that my t-shirt bristles. As though I have two hearts. As though I have two separately beating hearts. I watch for dead babies on the ceiling *a la Trainspotting*. None are forthcoming. I suppose this is a good sign, though I admit to a vague sort of disappointment, a sense that my suffering may have less validity than it would if it were depicted onscreen.

Maybe I should have stayed in Toronto. Maybe chasing after some movie concept wasn't the most practical of ideas. Maybe believing in a man who was never particularly reliable in the first place wasn't so smart. Though I've been single for four years now—*four years!* If I don't start to believe in someone soon, will I ever?

My jaw is painfully clenched. I remember to unclench it and then I forget and it clenches again. And then I remember again, because my chin is jammed up so tight against my molars that my whole skull aches.

I unclench.

This cannot be good for my heart.

Left.

Right...

I forget and then I remember and then I forget again.

The Londoner told me his name, but you'll have to forgive me for not mentioning it here; I'm trying very bravely to block it out.

As you might well imagine, the Londoner lives in London. Although I am forced to admit that I mean London, Ontario rather than London, England, and that the Canadian city has—it goes without saying—way less cachet than its counterpart across the pond.

He is stocky. He is freckled. He has ginger-colored hair and a fantastic set of choppers. He might be described as marginally attractive. But not by me.

We originally met at my farewell bash in Toronto through some mutual friends, though I could barely recall him by the time he arrived in Budapest as I was quite out of my mind at that going-away party, more than a little stunned by the idea of so completely leaving my life, such as it was, behind. (And even more stunned by the idea of abandoning said life for some Yankee named Jack who I screwed by chance back when I was twenty-two.)

The Londoner told me he was attending a conference in Prague in a few weeks. He told me Prague was about as far from Budapest as London, Ontario was from Toronto. He told me he had never been to Hungary. We were both consuming preposterous amounts of rye whiskey. I admit I may have led him on. I admit I may not have mentioned Jack. I admit I may have been covering my bases. I admit I took down his e-mail address.

But it was never the plan to actually invite him. It was never the plan to get stood up and then wander around and around and around Budapest's tourist attractions where I was constantly surrounded by international couples whose very presence was an awful reminder of *just how alone I was*, until I began to feel so desperately lonely that I deliberately typed in the Londoner's e-mail address and entreated him to visit me here 'for as long as his schedule might allow.'

Not until Jack bailed, that is.

Not until no other options presented themselves, that is.

Not until *Monsieur Parfait* left town on the Orient Express, that is.

For each of the four days that I saw him, the Londoner wore faded blue jeans and dully colored t-shirts bearing the logos of Canadian universities: U of T, U of Vic, Trent U, Dalhousie.

"I collect university t-shirts," the Londoner said.

"I own a Jeep," the Londoner said.

"I love hockey," the Londoner said. "Hockey is my life."

Which came as a startling blow. Regardless of loneliness, regardless of rye intake, I have one rule: I do not date hockey jocks. (The explanation perhaps for my four years of singledom. Or at least one of them.) Obviously, I'd been a bit pissed at my farewell bash.

Then came the mockery.

"It's just not right," he said about every foreign word, gesture, product, custom, until I thought my head might explode all over his stupid Canadian t-shirt collection.

And so in the name of quashing any romantic interest he might have held for me—and also to avoid directly stating my complete disinterest in him—I cleverly and almost immediately began to act like a lunatic.

To wit: I drank myself blind and near-drooling for three consecutive evenings; I suffered from an extended and unpleasant, though wholly imaginary menstrual cycle; I ended up in the middle of the dance floor at Old Man's (where I had actually hoped I might run into the Frenchman again) necking indiscreetly with some devilishly skinny English-as-a-Second-Language teacher, a 'just not right' Brit whom the Londoner swiftly dubbed 'the TESL wanker'; I performed a snuffling I-like-you-but-I'm-bad-news-but-I-like-you manic moment in his ridiculously swank and over-priced and inconveniently-located hotel room; I made banal observations in a tourist restaurant where all the other nearby tables stopped speaking in order to listen to my atrociously North American and offensively banal comments; I made fun of his lame-ass t-shirt collection; and then worst of all, during an unbearable conversational lull, I blathered on about women's issues and such, which I don't even, for the record, believe in.

But apparently it was not enough.

"Do you think we'll ever fuck?" the Londoner asked me on the final afternoon of his visit.

And opening my mouth to respond, I found that I was plumb out of excuses. I found that there was no more (contrived) lunacy in my repertoire. Nor was there a valid reason to deny sexual rewards to a man I myself had entreated to join me here, a man who had travelled all that way (though Prague isn't really all that far when you think about it) and at all that expense (though it's not like I recommended he check into an over-priced and inconveniently-located hotel) to see such an idiotic, though identically passported and therefore 'just about right' girl.

That's me.

"Do you think we'll ever fuck?"

No one else had ever lasted this long. No one else had even glimpsed the horizon of Day Two.

And so I found I had *no choice* but to resort to Jack.

The Londoner stared blank-faced into his 'just not right' mug of beer as I told him the story, or at least the important bits of the story. And even before I got to the end, even before I got halfway through, I began to realize that Jack was the real reason. He was the reason why this Londoner failed to interest me *so completely*. Jack was also the reason I'd hardly blinked an eye when *Monsieur Parfait* had departed—rather hastily, in retrospect—to catch the Orient Express back to Paris. Or so he told me. Though in all fairness, a savage hangover that didn't seem particularly amenable to movement—not even blinking— may have contributed to my indifference. Still, Jack *was* the real reason. The reason was Jack.

(You'd think I'd have figured it out earlier, like on the plane to Budapest, just for example. But I didn't. I hadn't. Perhaps the in-flight movie distracted? How I miss the heavenly balm of television.)

When I got to the end of the story, the Londoner said: "First the TESL wanker, now this."

I smiled indulgently. The Londoner was taking great pleasure in reminding me of my dance floor indiscretion with the Brit—for which I was truly sorry.

"Ya know, if I found the love of my life again after seven years," the Londoner said. "I wouldn't dick around on the internet for ten months."

I stared at his t-shirt. The giant *M* reminded me of my precarious ceiling.

"I'd be on a plane," he said. "Hell, I'd drive there in my Jeep."

"Seven months," I replied with a strange smile, still staring at his somehow fake-looking t-shirt.

The Londoner muttered: "Whatever."

And immediately, mercifully, *finally* I sensed the withdrawal of this small and unpleasant man's desire. Still, I couldn't help but add: "And I never said He was the love of my life."

The Londoner's eyes snapped onto mine then. He smiled. "No," he said. "No, you didn't say that, did you?"

And of course I was the first to look away.

Meeting Jack was an accident. Well, maybe not so much an accident as a slow-burning sickness; after all, here I am almost eight years later with new symptoms on the go.

The night we met, I was staring down what may have been the pinnacle of my youthful inebriation. (Seems to be a bit of a pattern—even now, well past my youth.) Remarkably, I was still capable of navigating the ground beneath me, and of hailing a taxi, and of finding the dance floor, thanks perhaps to routine and memory and maybe even olfactory impulses rather than anything resembling motor skills.

Once safely inside my club, I watched sanguine lights zigzag frantically across the walls. They made me queasy. I was borderline queasy. But then that was the desired state upon arrival, my own special brand of carefully contrived euphoria. (Because I was a student and I partied all the damn time and I could barely afford to buy even one drink once I got there.)

This was so many years ago.

There was no one else on the floor, but I danced anyway. The music boomed. There was lots of room to move, so I closed my eyes and started to spin and spin and spin. My favorite song came on and everything was so loud and so dark and so *right* I felt I might split into pieces with the sheer fucking joy of it all. I didn't mind—just so long as it didn't stop.

This was my high. This was totally how I got high.

When the song ended, I opened my eyes and lifted my head. I remembered where I was. I felt lucky to still be in one piece. And then I saw Him. (Though it is only in retrospect that He earns the capital.)

It was His concentration, His confidence, maybe even the easy lean of His body up against that speaker that caught my eye. Or maybe He was just the closest and me being so high, I couldn't be bothered to look around. Whatever. I went right up to Him. I went for Him straightaway.

"Can I have a kiss?" I yelled at Him over the harsh music, because this was how music and rye and dancing made me feel.

He stared at me without so much as a blink.

Up close He was pasty skin and blond clumps of hair—dirty-looking in a good way. I sensed a body that was thicker than I usually went for, but it was encased in black, and in the flashing-light darkness of the club I couldn't be sure. I stared at His face. There was something off-balance about Him, something that made you squint your eyes and look harder. He was completely still, yet He seemed to be moving at the same time. He stood there, watching me.

I felt caught, foolish, afraid, game, *ready*.

From behind His hair came a crooked, sly smile. I saw then that even His mouth was off-balance, the perpetual curve of a sneer. I shivered as He took my hand.

Still He said nothing.

He led me away from the dance floor, and through the churning lights. He walked me past the bar and towards the slim staircase. On the way up, we passed a pony-tailed girl who asked her friend why all the music here was so angry. I couldn't see His face. I would have liked to have seen His face. Did the sneer spread? He held the door open for me and then led me to an unlikely piece of concrete jutting up from the sidewalk across the street. There He let go of my hand.

We sat down.

He sparked up a cigarette, pulled out a mickey of Silk Tassel from inside His coat pocket and passed it to me. I took a sip and passed it back. He looked at me. He kept on looking at me.

I didn't move. I was twenty-two. I felt unsure, speechless, breathless, excited. I waited.

Finally He said: "I'm an American."

And so I laughed. I said: "Okay." The night was cool. I pulled my miniskirt down a little. I said: "I'm Canadian."

He waved a hand at the Toronto skyline. "I figured."

I took the cigarette He held out to me. I inhaled deeply. I watched Him watch me do it. I got dizzy. I got light-headed. I got a nicotine rush.

"It upsets some people," He said. "Americans."

I nodded. His voice was deep, sexy, and even though it was loud, it almost made you strain to hear it. I had no idea what the hell He was talking about. I could hear the music from inside the club. My knees jiggled. I was really drunk. I wondered if this conversation seemed strange because I was so very drunk.

He tilted His head. His sneered mouth tilted with it. "I like the way you dance."

I smiled. I wanted to go back inside, wanted to dance. I danced because I had to, but that didn't mean I wasn't embarrassed.

"You're a good dancer."

I kept smiling, though it seemed obvious He was making fun. No one else had ever suggested such a thing. Could such a statement be even partially true? But I was far too drunk to probe for sincerity.

Kiss me, I thought. Just fucking kiss me already.

Across the street, the door to the club banged open. It was made, appropriately enough, out of heavy metal. It banged hard. I jumped and twisted my head. Angry music spewed out around a woman framed in the doorway. She wore all black. She wore stilettos. She wore an expression that said: *I am totally pissed off.* She turned her head this way and that.

"Shit," I heard Him say, but it seemed to come from some distant locale.

And when I turned back to Him, He was gone. I turned my head this way and that, but I saw no one. There wasn't anyone to see.

Looking down at the ground beside me, I spotted the mickey of Silk Tassel. It had a sip left in it. Beside it lay half a cigarette, still burning. I picked up the mickey and drained it, contemplated the cigarette, then decided against it.

I walked back to the club and pushed past the pissed-off woman in stilettos. I almost fell down the stairs. Then I nearly threw up. But somehow I managed to find the dance floor again and dance it off. I sobered up a little and watched for Him. But I didn't see Him and then I started to forget what He even looked like—beyond the tilt, beyond the notion of something off-balance, beyond the something moving but still.

The first thing He said to me was: "I'm an American."

Stiletto Woman stood at the bar for a few songs then disappeared.

I danced.

Kiss me, I thought. Just fucking kiss me already.

But He didn't come back.

Exactly one week later, the following Thursday, I poured myself back into my club. It was no big deal. I was there every Thursday. But I didn't figure He'd be there. I figured He was American. I figured He was back in the land of the free and the home of the brave. And more importantly, I figured He had a girlfriend in black stilettos.

Leaning on a post near the dance floor, I sipped on a rye and waited for some decent music. I watched the crowd and I don't think that He crossed my mind even once. A week later, the whole encounter felt less significant than a dream—barely amusing, explanation-defying. And besides, I was twenty-two, such encounters were frequent, expected almost.

But when I felt the hand on my arm, I absolutely *knew* it would be Him. I turned around. I recognized Him straightaway—that unkempt hair, that crooked grin, that confidence.

He leaned in close to me.

I smelled something salty and...well something profoundly salty. It made my knees squishy. I shivered.

He said: "Don't I owe you a kiss."

It wasn't a question.

I said nothing. I was immobilized by His scent and the authority of His fingers sliding down the length of my arm and into my hand. I just stood there, blinking at Him.

Such authority!

Such focus!

Such hair!

I hardly even noticed as He once again led me away from the dance floor, through the lights and the crowd, past the long bar, and up the perilous staircase. He preceded me out onto the street and then put His lips to my ear.

He whispered: "Which way is home?"

I shivered. I felt His hand, His breath. I felt caught, foolish, afraid, game, ready. I felt *no alternative*, no choice. I said: "North. Due North."

He smiled then and raised an arm. He yelled: "Taxi!"

I breathed deep. I breathed as deeply as I could. I knew I was in trouble. Even then.

It felt, it felt, *it felt*.

With Him, even that first night, I didn't know what was going on. I was lost, confused. I was completely off-balance. I was not in charge. I was out of control. I was so satisfied. He was *so satisfying*. He was unpredictable and fucking fantastic. Unprecedented to say the least. Heady, exhilarating, unreal, *too real*, to expound slightly.

I didn't know what to say. I didn't know where I was. I didn't know why. Most of all there was no why. I discovered that the feeling He gave me of no choice, no alternative brought with it a strange surrender—strange because so undramatic and comfortable. I had no idea that I might take comfort in relinquishing control—it seemed so outdated, so girlish, so pre-the-women's-movement.

But a few hours later, with the sun fully up and the on-ramp to sobriety not so very far away, I got scared. That smell. That salty smell was everywhere. It made me dizzy, helpless. Residual vibrations from the evening's activities were still ping-ponging through the air. I couldn't think, couldn't breathe. He was lying right next to me—a long white back that demanded my attention, looking strong and vulnerable and too intimate in the hot light of day. I coveted. I coveted *hard*. I got the shakes. I got a visual of Stiletto Woman and her face said: *I am so pissed off.*

I turned away from His pale skin, and mumbled: "Don't you have somewhere you gotta be?" But inside, all I could think was: Don't go!

There was a long moment of nothing, during which time I wondered if He'd heard me; I didn't think I'd be able to repeat myself. I didn't breathe. Then He hoisted Himself up and began to gather His clothes. He eyed me while He put them on, that crooked smile peeking out from behind His tangled blond hair. I was relieved as each layer found its way onto His body. His bare skin was too much to deal with—I couldn't think.

I pulled on a t-shirt. I fidgeted. I thought: *Don't go!*

We stood at the door. He touched my hand. He said: "Where am I?"

I smiled, said: "Canada."

He laughed. We stood there. I fidgeted.

"I'll be at the club next Thursday," He said.

I said nothing. I thought: *Please don't go!*

He opened the door. He walked out.

I called after Him. I said: "Wait."

He stopped. He turned around.

I said: "I don't even know your name." (This is definitely a pattern.) It was a lame thing to say. I was twenty-two.

He smiled and said: "It's not so important." With a wink, He disappeared down the hall.

I shut the door and immediately wished He hadn't gone. I surveyed the morning-after debris and allowed myself a small smile, but then a moment later I was terrified. I'd never surrendered before—not like that anyway, not with such conviction. And the weirdest part, the worst part was that standing there, staring at the damage, feeling the vibrations slow and settle, it occurred to me that I could feel His absence more than I could feel my own presence.

It was scary. I was scared out of my mind. Even then. And that was only the first night.

Sometimes I wonder who I was before I met Jack. Or what I used to think about. Or what I used to do. I knew as soon as He left that morning that things weren't ever going to be the same. And I was right. In fact, everything I've ever done since that day, even the tiniest, most insignificant acts—like flossing my teeth or choosing which route to take to work or deciding which nightclub to frequent—*the totality of my entire life for the past seven and a half years* has been undeservedly significant. Significant because integral to my connection—past, present and future—with Him. Because it was all about trying to locate Jack, to attract Jack back to me, to run into Jack, to keep up appearances for Jack, to lure Jack back, to find Jack, *to end up with Jack.*

Though I am only now consciously admitting it. Though I have never admitted it before—even to myself. Because it just makes me feel so ashamed, so *not* a modern, independent woman. To be honest, I wish I'd never realized it at all.

Why didn't I splurge on a room with a television, for pity's sake?

Jack.

Supposedly, in a few days, His 'unexpected, unavoidable delay' will be sorted out (finally) and He will get on a plane and meet me here in Hungary, a total of five weeks late.

It is June 18th. I'm lying in a cracked room in Budapest, near-catatonic (or so I like to think), near-broken (reality) and I'm on hour nineteen of my responsibility-seeking nicotine withdrawal and I confess I do not entirely believe that Jack will *ever* show. It is possible that Jack will in fact stand me up again. And perhaps forever. Because this is exactly the kind of thing that Jack has always done to me.

But what's a girl to do when everyone else—even a Frenchman—is a big, fat dud compared to the possibility of a man I haven't seen in just years and years?

No really, I'm asking: What am I to do?

"Jack," He said the following Thursday. "The name's Jack."

"Who's the girl in the stilettos, Jack?" (I'd vowed to be strong.)

He smiled crookedly. "Nobody."

I did not smile back. I did not exude craving. I did not shriek: "I surrender!"

"Nobody anymore," He said.

I stared at Him hard.

He touched my arm. (That authority!)

He kissed my cheek. (Those lips!)

He flicked His hair. (Uncle!)

"Anna," I said. "My name's Anna."

I was twenty-two. And it turned out I wasn't very strong at all.

It's difficult for me to remember the beginning, to remember the good times, eclipsed as they've been by what happened after. Sometimes I wonder if there was any initial happiness at all.

The problem was that Jack and I never planned our meetings. We never exchanged practical information like last names or employment histories or family politics. We never even swapped telephone numbers. Because Jack didn't believe in 'that bourgeois obligation shit.' And so it was always just so frustratingly uncertain. But then I recall the confidence of His hands, the sureness of His lips, and it all comes back to me. A feeling more than anything, a burgeoning pleasure in your guts—*I get it!*

I remember weird things. Like how right away He said, while staring unflinchingly into my eyes: "You're so angry. I love how angry you are." And another time: "How did you get so sad?" So that there was this pervasive feeling that here was someone who could see me, someone who was actually listening. And more than that, someone for whom I didn't have to pretend, someone who actually wanted me to be real, someone who thought the real me—angry and sad—*wasn't* a total disaster. (Clearly unprecedented.)

So of the beginning, the most that I can say is that there was a sense of time passing, a sense of anything not related to 'time with Him' receding into 'who-cares' territory, a sense of the two of us mapping out our routine. And so maybe that's where I need begin, maybe that is all that I can explain.

This was the Jack-and-Anna routine.

I'd be at a club. I'd be dancing. I'd never know if He was coming. I'd never tell Him where I'd be; even hints were frowned upon. But He was good at finding me. When He wanted to. So then there He'd suddenly be, leaning up against a speaker or a post. He always leaned while He watched me, everything about the guy was off-balance, crooked, not quite straight-up. And I'd want to go over to

----

Him, but I'd keep dancing instead. And He'd just stand there—still, but moving—and He'd make me feel like I was the only one on the floor. He watched me hungry, like He'd never seen the likes of me in all His life. He told me time and again that I was an amazing dancer. He said it with maximum awe. And this was a revelation. This was the opposite of everything I'd ever been told. This was the earth going from flat to round in under sixty seconds.

So I'd kick and flail and shake my ass with new abandon. I'd dance and dance and dance. I'd feel lighter and sexier and higher and hotter and more like my real self than I'd ever been. I wasn't pretending. The nights I saw Him were the only times in my life I wasn't penalized for not pretending. And I'd think: He may not know my last name, but He knows *this*. And no one else knows *this*.

Then we'd dance, almost together. We'd fight the floor and the air and the crowd. We'd do it for hours, right beside each other in the middle of a floor made slippery with broken glass and spilled liquor until the songs ran out and the lights came up and the spell was broken just a little. We'd stare at each other, panting and blinking through our dripping hair and the unflattering lights, and then we'd lock hands almost angrily and head north, due north, pushing and pulling and lurching through the brightening night streets. And we always went back to my place. And I always surrendered.

And the truth is, I got off on it. I got off on not knowing. I got off on being found. I got off on the uncertainty.

Even as it drove me *completely insane.*

Because though we saw more and more of each other, and though I tried my best to remain cool and detached and maybe even indifferent—because this seemed to be the reaction He was looking for—the plain truth of it was that it was never, ever enough as far as I was concerned.

I wanted more Jack. I wanted *way* more Jack.

My friends were outraged. "He hasn't even given you His *number?*"

And I guess I didn't do a very good job of explaining Jack's theories, because they just raised their eyebrows and made gasping fish-out-of-water noises. They didn't seem to understand that it was a completely out-of-my-control kinda thing.

I was not in control.

Find me, I found myself thinking. I thought it all the time. I couldn't *stop* thinking it. And most of the time He did. He almost always did. But sometimes He didn't. And when that happened, there was nothing I could do—no number to call, no last name to curse, no place of business to harangue. Just me, too-drunk and alone at some determined nightclub, desperately scanning the crowd until all that remained was a whole evening's worth of Not-Him's.

And I'd dance and dance and dance. I'd spin in desperate circles, spinning round and round and round. But it was never the same. It was never even close to the same. All the old voices surfaced. All the old voices jeered and pointed and shrieked: "The earth is flat, freak-girl! The earth is flat!" And I believed them. Without Him around, I totally believed them.

And inevitably, the night would end with the same persistent thought: It's like no one even knows I'm here. Like without Him, they can't see me at all, never mind see me the way He does. It's like I'm all wrong all over again.

And it would be everything I could do just to drag my weary body back home, like I was dragging all those Not-Him's through the dark streets behind me, a whole dance club full of disappointment—an unbearably heavy load.

Personal epiphany number two (which is about as welcome as the I'm-an-idiot revelation): I'm pretty sure that this is

---

it for me. Yes, it's obvious that Jack is my last shot. If Jack isn't the one, then maybe there is no one.

Because I'm almost thirty.

Because by traveling all the way to Hungary to see this guy, I've not only put myself on the line, but well past it, and if things don't work out, I shan't be approaching said line again.

Because I refuse to date anyone who's into hockey and as a Canadian this eliminates ninety per cent of the male population. And of the remaining ten per cent, how many can possibly be straight?

Leaning lewdly over my bathroom sink, I stare at myself. I see blue eyes. I see parched pink lips. I see eyebrows that could stand a thorough grooming. I see my face, still this same oval face that is just so maddeningly average, and maybe even below average at this moment, this particularly low moment in my life.

I notice that my roots are now quite out of control, quite unruly, quite incorrect ratio-wise, quite a total of five-weeks-and-six-days long. My roots, I realize, while staring into the spotted mirror of my dingy, fluorescent, Hungarian bathroom with my heart twitching irregularly inside of my chest in a Morse-code plea for nicotine, my roots are very much in need of servicing.

My fingers twist and pull at the skin on my face. My average, and maybe even below average at this particularly low moment, nose stretches wider and wider. It never used to be this wide. It never used to look this way. My face is the same and yet completely different. I don't even remember what I used to look like. I hardly even remember who I used to be.

It is hour twenty-two of my stupefying nicotine withdrawal. My jaw clenches. My t-shirt twitches.

And then I remember: This is the one that has to work. This is it. Jack is it. And then I wish I'd never realized it at all. Because I don't even know where that asshole *is* right now, never mind who I used to be, who *we* used to be.

This cannot be good for my heart. What kind of permanent damage am I doing to my heart?

I stare at the gift, the 'oh-my-god-we're-reunited' gift I have bought for him and which I have carefully placed on a small table across the room from my hideous Hungarian chair-bed. It is wrapped in a garish red print. The ribbon is white. You cannot imagine uglier packaging than this. But I did not protest to the Hungarian shop-girl who picked out these colors for me, mostly because I was too tired to argue in sign language. But despite its packaging, it is a thoughtful gift. I have known I would get it for Him for months. When I finally see Jack again, I thought, I know what to buy for Him.

And I did.

But now I remember, I have just remembered, He isn't even into gifts. He says I'm gift enough.

Or at least He said so a long time ago.

A specific flash.

It was close to Christmas. We were naked and drunk in my room, my student dormitory room. There were permanent globs of ice affixed to the thin windowpane. I was happy. I was always so happy when we were together, but not in an exuberant way, more like in a calm certainty kind of way. And whenever He found me, that calm certainty obliterated all of the previous disappointments and frustrations and Not-Him's—no matter how numerous or intense.

But my friends had made me promise.

"Maybe you should give me your number," I said. "Just in case."

He didn't even look up. "In case of what?"

"In case I need to get ahold of you."

There was an unruffled silence, then: "I don't really have a permanent number."

I smiled to show my complete lack of annoyance, but I didn't give up. "You going anywhere for the holidays?"

He sucked on a cigarette. "Don't know."

"I'm going home," I said. "Fucking nightmare, but I have to."

He stared at the wall behind my head. He didn't ask me where home was, nor did He identify His.

"Flin Flon, Manitoba," I laughed. "That's *my* fucking home."

He stubbed out His cigarette. He didn't laugh.

I persisted. "You a fan of the holidays?"

He shrugged, rubbed my leg.

I wanted to know everything. I knew nothing. I quite literally knew Jack. And twenty-five. And American. And Sagittarius. I knew it was Sagittarian season, so I said: "When's your birthday, Sag man? Did I miss it already?"

He shook His head, staring determinedly downwards at the mauled bed sheets.

"I wanna buy you a gift."

He sighed wearily. "Don't. I don't believe in gifts. You're gift enough."

My voice got soft. "Ya know, I've been thinking. Maybe you and I should—"

His eyes snapped fiercely onto mine. He curled His lopsided lip into more of a condescending sneer than usual. He said: "Should?"

Blushing, caught, I shut my mouth and freed my eyes. I stared at a spot on the sheets. I didn't look back at Him for a very long time. I heard Him light another cigarette.

I thought: Well that wasn't very nice.

I thought: The honeymoon is definitely over.

I thought: No big deal, I can change Him.

Then, running a flat hand through the air above my futon, He said: "I can feel all of your lovers, you know." He looked up at me slyly. "Your bed vibrates in the night."

This was years ago.

I was only twenty-two.

My head spun. I wondered if He was fishing. I wondered how much He really knew. I wondered if He was finally getting interested in some kind of personal disclosure. So I smiled confidently and changed the subject.

The feeling of His lovers was a little more concrete. It came a few days later in the form of the clap.

Jack and I rode the Airport Bus together. It was Christmas. I was off to see my family—the last time I ever traveled anywhere to spend the holidays with them, so you can just imagine how well that went. Jack was along for the ride. I told Him He needn't bother.

"You don't have to," I said, ever conscious of our commitment against the evils of obligation and appropriation and compromise.

"I want to," He'd replied.

We were both on tetracycline, for which I knew I was supposed to be furious. But to be honest I wasn't as mad as I was supposed to be.

Toronto was gray and dingy. It was late December.

When we got to the terminal I had time to spare. Instead of leaving, Jack bought us each a cup of coffee and we sat down. Something unsettled hung between us. I didn't know what was going on. I'd never felt this quiet earnestness between us before. He'd never bought me even a cup of water before. Neither of us spoke really—what more needs be said when you're sharing an STD?

Then He handed me a Christmas present across the bolted-down table. I was surprised. I blustered on about not having a gift for Him. He didn't seem concerned. When I opened the gift, I found a black woolen tuque with a cartoon skull-and-crossbones knit into it. Very Jack, I thought. Very goth. And I wondered if He was serious.

I was twenty-two. Amazingly, I was an even bigger idiot then than I am now.

When I asked Him if He'd made it Himself, He said no, and then I felt rude for asking. I had nothing for Him, because He had told me quite specifically that He didn't believe in gifts. And besides, what material item could possibly represent my feelings—plural and ever-changing and now infected—for Him?

I got up to go and we kissed and He gave me a long hug. That thing hung between us even then. Still, we didn't really speak. He hugged and hugged and hugged me.

All the way to Manitoba, I stared at the tuque and thought that maybe we'd turned a corner, maybe He really did want to be with me after all. And I spent the entire 'vacation' talking about Him surreptitiously—that was the only way really—to my older sister, who looked baffled and more than a little appalled, especially when she saw the tetracycline.

On the journey back, while wandering around the Winnipeg airport between flights, I saw a sleek silver liquor flask. It reminded me of the mickey Jack always kept in His pocket, so I bought it for Him as a belated gift. Problem was I had no clue when I'd run into Him again, and no way to contact Him, so I took to carrying it around with me all the time. My apprehension increased each day as I waited for Him to appear, but it was the middle of January before it finally happened. And when I showed Him the gift He was shocked. Turns out, He'd considered the whole airport scene a final farewell for us.

"What did you think the tuque was about?" He asked, leaning back against a club wall.

But I just thought He was being a bit goth. I didn't think He meant it literally. And besides, a few hours later we ended up back at my place.

Things were never really over for Jack and I.

Cigarette, cigarette, cigarette, cigarette, cigarette, cigarette, cigarette, cigarette, cigarette, cigarette, cigarette, cigarette, cigarette...

Flash.

Sometime after this—probably a Thursday or a Friday considering that it happened at Catch-22—I was pretending not to be waiting for Him, but glancing through the dark whenever I remembered Him, which, let's face it, was all the time. It was late. Later than He usually showed. I figured it wasn't going to happen.

I tried not to think of Him. I tried not to think of His hair or His skin or His authoritative hands or His lopsided grin. I tried not to think about how much I looked forward to seeing His body leaned up against some massive speaker, His blond hair shining dully beneath the lights. I tried not to think how lost I felt when He wasn't around. (Though this was the least of the concessions I would end up making with Him, for Him, around Him—I'm in Budapest, Hungary, for god's sake!)

But the truth is that He was all I ever thought about.

The Sugarcubes' *Birthday* came on. It was my favorite song. I danced. When the song ended I paused long enough to determine that the next tune was crap, then I headed to the bathroom. On the way there a hand reached out from the darkness. It was Jack. It was a suddenly materialized Jack.

"You're here," I said. Unnecessarily.

"Came to tell you I'm hanging at a new club."

"A new club?"

"Just down the street. A DJ I know."

"I'll come."

I said it immediately.

"No, no, I know you love it here. Stay. I just didn't want you to wait on me."

Which seemed to negate the concepts that Jack and I (mostly Jack) were still claiming we were about, or rather what we were not about: obligation, appropriation, compromise, last names.

"I'll come. Let's go."

And I could not tell if He was pleased or pissed off, but He did take me there. He avoided the main roads. He avoided the lights. He led me through back alleys I'd never been down. I lost my sense of direction and just followed Him.

We did not touch each other, nor did we speak. I felt a distinct sense of change, almost a loss of power—though let's face it, I never had much. I've left my clubs now, I thought. I've left my circuit. I'm walking into His world now. This is His world. And of course as soon as we got there the DJ was great. And we danced and we drank and everything seemed somehow better: louder, faster, sharper, cheaper. And I thought: Power? Who cares about power. That's not what it's about at all. And that night it was so completely clear to me that Jack and I were *meant* for each other. Even with the bullshit. Maybe because of the bullshit. Because I was just so sickeningly happy, so blissed-out and *sure*.

Until the very end of the night, that is. Until we got near my place and I was fumbling through my pockets for my keys.

It was the middle of winter. It was approximately one hundred below zero without the wind chill factored in. We were twenty feet from my door when He stopped.

47

I turned to Him impatiently. "Jack, it's freezing." I was shivering. I was bouncing up and down in some sort of futile attempt to create body heat. And also because I needed to pee quite desperately.

And He said: "I'm not coming in with you."

And He said: "I'm leaving Toronto tomorrow."

And He said: "I don't know when I'll be back."

And smoke billowed out of His mouth as He spoke and everything suddenly seemed just *so much worse than it had ever been.*

My head goes round and round in circles. Does your head do that?

Like I just lie here at the twitchy age of twenty-nine, on the twenty-ninth hour of this tenacious physical withdrawal, and I stare at my cracked ceiling and the same things run round and round my brain.

Should I meet Jack? Should I not meet Jack? Should I go back to Canada? Should I not go back to Canada? And if I do, what the hell will I tell them about Jack?

Should I get my roots done here or try to hold out for my colorist Marla back in Toronto instead? Should I shower? Should I not shower? Should I just grow up and go home and grovel for my old job back? (Accounting, if you must know.) Is there any way to grow up without humiliating groveling?

Should I have a cigarette? Should I not have a cigarette? Should I make a cup of coffee or will that make me want to smoke even more? Should I inform some kind of authority figure about this cracked ceiling? But then who would care and just who exactly is in charge here anyway?

Do you think He'll still be attracted to me? And what if He's not? What if He sees me and realizes He's made a terrible mistake? Is this something I want to know? And what part of me is He actually looking for? Do I even still have that part after six, seven, almost eight years? Would I even recognize it as something I *used* to have? Or what if He's an ugly old fat man now? What then?

Wouldn't it be safer *not* to meet Him, to keep the dream alive? Or is the dream already dead and I'm the only one who doesn't know it?

I am twenty-nine.

My name is Anna Woods.

I used to be an accountant, but now I'm just a girl idiot on the twenty-ninth hour of a debilitating withdrawal from nicotine and I am so fucking scared. *Because I'm relying on a completely unreliable man.* Even if He is the one I think about fondly when I'm firmly ensconced in the permanent sag of my futon, lonely and alone in the middle of the night, attempting to conjure up some sort of evidence that I ever interacted with other human beings at all, even so, He's not the sort of man a girl ought to *rely* on.

And if my excuse, my last resort, my lost love finds me but doesn't want me after all, then what am I left with? What could I possibly hope for then?

Please Jack. Please come for me. I am so unbelievably frightened. I am so close to losing all hope. I am so close to losing all my faith in you.

Jack.

Please...

Wherever He went, He went for five weeks and two days. Somewhere in the middle of March, on the afternoon of the thirty-seventh day of His inexplicable and abrupt absence, I walked out of my front door and there He was.

"Is it ever good to see you," He said. He looked more frantically still than usual.

I hurried past Him. "I'm late for class," I said, even though things like attendance and learning did not concern me—especially not when Jack was around. But I'd been doing some thinking while He was gone. I'd been doing thirty-seven days worth of thinking. Like about how I didn't even know His last name. Like about how I didn't have so much as a temporary phone number for Him. Like about how I might have seen Stiletto Woman at the bar we went to the last night we were together. And just who in the hell did He get the clap from anyway?

He hurried to catch up with me. "I missed you."

"I gotta go."

"Stay."

"I gotta go." I pulled away from Him and walked faster. He stopped. He let go.

I went to class. I took notes. I took half-hearted notes. I thought: Why didn't I stay?

A friend took pity on me, took me out for pitchers of Canadian. I raged about Him. I said things like *the nerve* and *He wishes* and *what an asshole* and *thirty-seven days*. My friend listened. My friend nodded. My friend suggested we call it a night.

I walked home, weaving and stumbling. I concentrated hard on the upcoming ground. Maybe I even sniffled a little. It was only as I approached my front door that I looked up. It was almost dark, but I saw immediately that it was Him, His body leaning casually against a faded newspaper box, His dirty hair gleaming.

He said: "I missed you. I missed you like crazy."

"Fuck you."

He was calm. He said: "Fuck you too honey."

I glared at Him. I gave Him the evil eye.

But He just stared back at me like He stared in the clubs: *He saw me.* I was *so* addicted to that look.

I said: "Don't call me honey, asshole."

He gave me a crooked smile. The air around Him sizzled.

I opened the door and stood there. He brushed past me and took my hand and led us both inside. But before I could even get to the beer fridge, Jack shrugged off His jacket and thrust out His left forearm at me. It was covered in gauze.

"Check this out," He said.

I stood quietly while He peeled off the bandage and held out His limb to me for inspection. The skin looked red, manhandled, raw. There was a comical patch of hairless rectangle halfway between wrist and elbow. In the center of this was a tattoo which read: I♥NY. I wasn't sure what reaction He was looking for, so I said: "Is that where you went?"

He snorted. "I wish."

"You from there?"

"Nope. Can't say as I've ever been."

I looked down at the tattoo again. The ♥ was an enviable red. "I don't get it."

He started to reapply the gauze. "It's a marking," He said. "I'm marking the moment."

"What moment?"

He just smiled. "It's just such a cool fucking logo too, you know? Just like basic and...cool."

I moved towards the fridge. I wasn't sure I even wanted His story anymore.

"What moment?" I asked again.

"Born and raised in Seattle."

I passed Him a beer and took a long sip of my own. Staring at Him, seeing how pleased He was with Himself, I had a fleeting moment of clarity. This person is an idiot, I thought. How is it possible that I am so smitten by this idiot?

Taking a deep breath, I said: "What're you doing here then? Seattle's totally the place to be, right?"

"Seattle's done."

I raised my brows.

"Finished," He said. "Plus my sister."

I paused. "You have a sister?"

"Sure. She married some scumbag Canuck who fucked off on her and the kids. I came to the rescue." He frowned. "Why else would I come here?"

I shook my head. I really didn't know. I waited for more. Did I want more? Anyway, none was forthcoming, so I said: "You know it's kinda uncool to get a tattoo of a city you've never been to."

He looked right through me. "I totally disagree."

"Well it is."

"Says you."

"What's your point?"

He grabbed for His bag. "Hey, lemme take your picture. I'm taking up photography. I think it's my calling. Just a coupla nude shots to get warmed up."

"Yeah that's gonna happen."

"Just one."

"No! Aah-ha-ha! Stop! Rape!"

There was a brief struggle, but He had my arms pinned in a matter of seconds. His face hovered just above my own; lanky locks of blond tickled my cheeks. We were both panting.

"C'mon, Anna. Play nice," He cooed. "I missed you, you know. Thought about you the whole time I was gone."

I turned my face away from His eyes, felt only a numbness, a dismayed numbness. I found myself staring directly at His bandage, which I saw had come loose in our struggle. One flap was hanging completely free of His skin. The 'T' and a portion of the red '♥' were visible.

"Just one little picture," He whispered. "You're so beautiful."

I found myself unable to look at Him, unable to move either. The red ink on His arm was mesmerizing.

"Was going to call you," He smirked, "but wouldn't you know it, I don't have your num–Aaaah!"

He leapt away from me. I looked down at my hand, saw the gauzy bandage clutched in my hand, blood and something black mashed beneath my nails. I was still filled with that numbness, that dismay. It seemed to be evolving into a deep despair.

"You bitch!" He screamed, clutching at His arm. There were deep red claw marks pouring down the length of it. His face was shock and fury. "You fucking bitch! What the fuck is your problem? Aaah, god, that fucking hurt! Are you fucking crazy?

I smiled a little despite the fact that I suddenly felt like throwing up. "Just marking the moment, baby. Just thought the moment needed some marking."

I was twenty-two.

I was stronger than I thought.

Generally speaking, the less Jack and I said to each other at this point the better. If we had to speak, we spoke about movies or music or superstars, because these were the things He suddenly believed in. Or I made fun of His being American and He let me, because that was the price of being number one and we both knew it.

But we still didn't exchange last names. Nor did we swap phone numbers. Nor did we explain, nor demand explanations for thirty-seven day absences.

We danced.

We drank.

We debauched.

Anything more and we were into an argument.

"Canadian pop culture totally sucks," He said. "Canadian pop culture does not exist."

We'd just walked by a poster for the Toronto International Film Festival. Jack was newly obsessed with pop culture. Jack had had a pop culture epiphany in His thirty-seven day absence.

"You are so American," I said. Because this was my stock response to Jack attacks. Because this was how Jack and I now lived: we mock-lived.

"It's true."

"Douglas Coupland. David Cronenberg. Tragically Hip."

Jack affected an innocent falsetto. "Who?"

I stared at Him. I wondered if He was right. I wondered if Canadian pop culture did suck. And then I wondered if I'd always thought this or if I was only thinking this because He'd just said so. But I didn't know the answer to this question. I don't think there is an answer to this question.

"You're such an asshole," I whispered. Because this was my other stock response to Jack attacks.

He stared at me. "And you're so *fucking nice*."

And still I stayed, still I surrendered. Because it was never ever about the words, was it?

Turned out He was in love with another girl.

I was twenty-two.

My name was Anna Woods.

Those days, Him finding me was the exception rather than the rule. Things were near the end. Things were always near the end for Jack and I. (Though never apparently over.)

"I'm having a party," He said. "You have to come."

"I do?"

"April 21st. You're not busy, right?"

"What's the occasion?" I asked, because this was the first time Jack had ever wanted to make plans.

"No occasion. Just a spring party."

"A party for spring."

He shrugged.

"Where?"

"My sister's." He hesitated, like He'd revealed too much. "I'll come get you, bring you there."

I thought: He really likes me now.

I thought: He finally wants to let me into His life.

I thought (get this): Maybe the party is for me.

He showed up at my place with a case of Canadian. He looked like He'd already had a few.

"Never show up too early for a party," He said, holding out a bottle.

I took it. "Even your own?"

"*Especially* your own. Bottoms up!" He drained His beer.

I took a small sip. I said: "Are you all right?"

He cracked a fresh one and leaned against my desk.

"Are you aware you're drinking a strong *Canadian* beer?"

He looked down at the bottle then. I glimpsed the foreshadowing of a double chin. He stared at the label, then He smirked at me. "Wouldn't have it any other way...would not have it otherwise."

I smiled uncertainly.

"So tell me who-all is going to be there."

"Who-all," He whispered, staring out the cab window. He'd turned sullen as soon as we'd stumbled out of my place and into the cab. "People are gonna be there, that's *who-all*."

"Yeah, well, will I like these people?"

He turned to me then. "Will *you* like them?" He laughed. He snorted. He fingered His I♥NY tattoo, which seemed to have survived the mauling. "The question is, honey, will they *like you*."

And I let Him say this to me. These are the sorts of things I let Him say.

We walked into the house. I had no idea where we were. I was drunk. I was completely off-balance. I was praying for a sudden infusion of charm.

Jack pulled aside a tall, stocky man just inside the door. Jack put a beer in my hand. Jack said: "This is Harry. Harry, Anna." Jack walked away.

"Hi Harry."

Harry said: "Are you the Canadian?"

I frowned. "How can you tell?"

"You're the only one I don't know."

I looked around the room. It was small and packed with people. There was a thick camaraderie in the air, a camaraderie which clearly did not include me. I said: "Everyone here is American?"

"Through and through."

"So what's the occasion? Some kind of *coup d'etat* I should know about?"

"Jack didn't tell you?"

I shrugged, sipped my beer.

"Fucking Jack, *eh*?" Harry said, nudging me hard in my left breast, though surely he must have been aiming for my ribs. "Never tells anyone anything. Center of the universe, that guy."

I felt borderline queasy.

"It's a celebration. Sabine just sold her first screenplay for some crazy amount of money. She flew us all up here for a party, said Jack missed us, said Jack was homesick." Harry paused. Harry looked me up and down. "Though looking at you, what's to miss?"

I blinked at him. I said: "Which one is Sabine?"

"Jack's *last* girlfriend," Harry rolled his eyes. "Oh you mean here?"

I felt faint.

Harry lifted his head. Harry scanned the crowd. Harry pointed the way. "Over there," he said. "Right beside Jack. She's the broad in the fuck-me stilettos."

It was late. It was a warm night. It was now an outdoor party.

I sat beside Him. I sat beside Him and I watched Him watch her. I sat beside Him and I watched Him watch her and I didn't say a thing, because Jack and I were not about saying anything—what could I say? I didn't even know His last name.

She wore stilettos. She wore an indecent miniskirt. She wore an expression that said: *I'm less pissed off than I used to be, but not by much.*

I looked at her close-up and saw a chronic right-eye twitch. She sat on a metal folding chair. The rest of us sat on the grass. He was at her feet. He gazed up at her. His back was almost turned to me. He longed for her. He admired her. The party was for her. The occasion was *her*. Any fool could see.

Harry sat on the other side of me. Harry was the only one who talked to me the whole night, as though I was invisible to the rest, as though I didn't even exist. "I'm really into this billboard thing now," Harry said to me.

I stared at Jack. Jack stared at Sabine.

"Billboard appropriation," Harry whispered. "You know, you take something established, something someone else paid for and put up, and then you claim it as your own, use it for your own purposes."

"Seattle is done," Sabine was saying. "Especially now that Kurt's dead. Finished. New York is where it's at now. I fucking love New York."

I stared at Jack. Jack gazed up at Sabine. I was pissed out of my head. I watched the twitch in the right eye of the girl He loved, and I thought: Surely this is a joke. This has got to be a joke. I looked around for the punch line. I looked around for someone to nudge, but I was being unilaterally ignored.

Sabine said: "Rock is out. Film is in." Her eye twitched.

I've been deliberately brought here, I thought. He has deliberately ensured that I am here, making plans as He never has before, bringing a case of Canadian beer as He never has before and now He's deliberately ignoring me.

I turned to Harry. I whispered: "What's Jack's last name? What's Jack's phone number?"

Harry laughed. "I like you. You're funny." He looked me over, lingering longer than necessary upon my chest. "You've got heart."

"Film's the new rock-n-roll," Sabine said. "It's the new photography, the new poetry, the new literature. Film is *it* man."

The grass was wet under my ass. Jack was looking up at Sabine like—no, I have taken great measures not to remember that look. I will *not* remember that look. But one thing was clear: things had changed since the night we'd met, the night He'd run away from her.

I reached out my hand to touch His leg. He ignored it, didn't even turn His head, didn't even bother to swat at it. And in turn, she barely acknowledged Him.

The whole thing was a joke.

I hated her, hated her indifference. She was still talking. She talked and talked and talked. How could anyone stand to be around such incessant babbling?

Still she droned on.

"For example, Canadian pop culture totally sucks," she said. "Canadian pop culture doesn't even exist."

I looked at Jack. Jack looked at Sabine.

Harry leaned over. Harry whispered: "No offence."

I turned to him. I looked at him like he was crazy. I gave him a look that said: I am so pissed off.

"Pop culture is like the only reflection we have of ourselves. Wait till you see my movie. This is totally the premise of my movie."

"Excuse me?" I said very loudly.

Everyone turned to me. Everyone gaped. Everyone narrowed their eyes.

"May I remind you"—I looked pointedly, if drunkenly, at each of them—"that you Yanks are on Canadian soil." I pressed my fingers into the ground and grabbed for a handful of dirt to back up my point, but the earth was still winterized. My hand came up scraped and frozen and clutching only a tiny bit of dirt and grass.

Everyone stared at me except her. She stared at the ground while her eye twitched.

I continued. "And it is common practice, at least among these parts, not to insult your host."

"Who is that?" someone whispered.

"The Canadian," someone hissed back.

"No one was insulting you," Sabine said, still staring at the ground. "You just don't have any good art."

I squeezed my paltry handful of dirt. "Says you."

She turned to me then. Her eye stopped twitching. I swear to god her eye stayed completely still. She whispered: "Exactly."

Jack stared at the ground. Jack just stared down at the ground. I watched. I waited. Nothing happened, so I stood

----

up, still clutching my dirt. I looked from her to Him, Him to her. I must have raised my hand, because Harry whispered: "Do it."

I opened my fingers. The earth fell. "And I guess since you're footing the bill," I said, weaving slightly on my feet. "You would be the host."

Sabine smiled. Her eye resumed its twitch.

I shook my hand. I shook my head. I shook it off. I said: "Thanks for the party." I walked into the empty house.

The conversation started up again behind me. Someone laughed.

I walked out the front door and I thought: This is it, honey. This is definitely it.

The streets were dark and silent but for the sound of my footsteps. I didn't know where I was, beyond east. When Jack had mumbled directions to the cab driver earlier in the night, all I'd caught was east. I wandered. I tried to decide which way was west. My Gazelles squawked intermittently against the dark pavement.

I was so defeated. I breathed complete and utter defeat. He'd deliberately brought me there so that He could abandon me. I was deliberately abandoned. And I didn't even get the point. What was the point? For me to leave? For me to get fed up and pissed off? For her to get fed up and pissed off?

Probably for me to fuck off.

And on top of it all, I'd forgotten to memorize the address. I'd planned to look for the phone and maybe a phone number while I was there, or at least mark down the address. But I'd forgotten. Though what did it matter if *this was it*?

I was so not familiar with those streets. I saw then that the road I was on ended at a park. A murky and unwelcoming park. There was no movement, no sign of life around me. The houses were dark. The cars were stationary. The park loomed silently ahead.

Her face, her face, her face.

She could not have been less bothered by my presence. I wasn't even *slightly* effective, so why bother bring—

And then it hit me. The whole thing was some kinda joke and for every joke there's a punch line. That goddamn punch line was me!

A low, growling sound seemed to be emanating from somewhere within the trees ahead. I turned around and walked back down the silent street I'd just crossed.

I thought: I am the punch line. I am the punch line. I am...

It was a low point. This is definitely one of my many low points. Of course it wasn't quite the end either. It was never the end—I could not end it!

Oh sure, I had trouble getting out of bed for awhile. I even stayed away from the clubs for awhile. But as soon as I went back, He was there. I knew He'd be there. And I knew I'd surrender.

The problem was, I couldn't give up that high so easily. I could never walk away. How do you walk away from someone like Him?

No really, I'm asking.

Why in the hell would I ever want to see this asshole again in the first place? Why would I ever want to be with someone like that? He's not even my type: blond and big— or maybe not so much big as not emaciated—and so goddamn overbearing to boot.

He's just so maddeningly attractive is all. He's just so goddamn intoxicating. And that hair...

My name is Anna Woods.

I am twenty-nine and I am on the fiftieth hour of my debilitating nicotine withdrawal and I have begun to imagine—no, I have begun to actually *see* my door handle turning.

Even though it is not. Even though it clearly is not.

I think this is the nervous breakdown part. Ceilings caving and door handles turning. I really cannot get out of this vile chair-bed. Even if I wanted to, even if I wasn't giving up the glory of the nicotine rush of which I am so very very fond. This is definitely some sort of nervous breakdown. My whole being, my whole body, the entirety of my mind is throbbing with misery.

Am I going to off myself? God, the idea has not crossed my mind in ages. Years maybe. Not since Flin Flon. Not since the immediate after-effects of growing up in Flin Flon, Manitoba dissipated. Though I admit, it did take a year or two.

I glare at the door handle. I am more than a little thrilled by the inherent drama of a good self-offing. But then I realize that no seriously suicidal person quits smoking right before they do themselves in. I mean really, what would be the point?

It is the middle of the night.

I can almost hear the ceiling split, have been almost hearing it for hours now. I turn the light on and fumble for my eyeglasses, my heart lurches as I peer sternly up at it, peer until I have assured myself, until I can convince myself that it is indeed intact. But then surely I would know. If it were really splitting that is. Surely I wouldn't require my eyeglasses to see that.

But as soon as the light is out, I swear to god I can actually hear the roof over my head breaking in two...

He kept me hanging on. He found me just often enough that I couldn't let go, and then right before my twenty-third birthday, He called me. He used the telephone.

I thought: How long have you had my number?

He said: "Don't make plans. I'm gonna take you out on your birthday, show you the time of your life."

I said: "What time are you picking me up?"

This was years ago.

I was turning twenty-three.

My birthday came. I played The Sugarcubes' *Birthday* over and over and over again in my dorm room while I waited for Him. I wore a new skirt, new shoes, cherry-tart red lipstick. I checked my watch. I pressed Rewind.

He got late. He got real late.

I poured myself a rye, drank it one gulp and poured another. It wasn't long before my lipstick was smeared across my face, wasn't long before I was shit-faced and defeated. Again. Because it was just so obvious that the bastard wasn't coming.

And still I waited for Him to call me.

(I was an even bigger idiot then than I am now. Frankly it's a small consolation.)

Hours later, I watched my clock flip over to midnight. I was so relieved that it was over.

I thought: Finally. It's over.

Then I laid down on my bed and felt absolute relief.

The next morning I woke up one hundred per cent hungover and one hundred per cent over Him.

I thought: What kind of fool am I?

I thought: What kind of sick fucker is He?

I thought: Fuck this shit for real.

And I meant it. I really did.

Of course one week later, He showed up at my door with flowers and a manila envelope. He said: "Happy Birthday!"

I said: "Are you out of your fucking mind?"

He lowered the flowers and leaned against the doorframe. He looked genuinely confused. Things swirled around Him though He was perfectly still.

For a moment, just a single moment, I believed Him. Then I said: "Get out. Just get the fuck away from me."

He frowned.

I slammed the door on His face. I stood there a moment, breathing hard, memorizing His skin, His hair, His perpetual sneer, memorizing the end—almost seeing Him through the fingerprint-smudged door.

This was the bravest thing I had ever done.

It was as I took an unsteady step back that the manila envelope skidded underneath the door. I stared at it, afraid. When I heard His footsteps recede, I picked it up. My hands shook.

Inside I found a single photograph. It was a blown-up glossy—8 x 10. In this photograph, I am sleeping. And naked. The sheets are rumpled, and though it looks as though there might recently have been someone lying beside me (Him presumably), that perhaps there even *should* be someone else in the bed with me (Him presumably), in the photograph I am alone and peaceful and content, as perhaps I can only be when I'm asleep. And perhaps also as I can only be when I'm in bed with Him.

I stared at the picture for a long time. I couldn't begin to imagine when this picture had been taken—certainly it was without my knowledge. I suppose I ought to have worried about the neg, worried about duplicates or additional shots. But I didn't. That wasn't what that picture was about. I slipped it back in its envelope and put it on a high and hard-to-reach shelf and tried to forget it, tried to forget Him.

Not long after, I threw out all the Jack bits that were scattered across my world: a book He'd once lent me, the skull-and-crossbones tuque, holed socks He'd never bothered to retrieve, half a pack of crushed Marlies, His Clamato juice for making morning-after Caesars which He claimed were a bona fide hangover cure and a profound contribution (Canadian apparently) to the world.

But I didn't throw out the photograph. I kept only the photograph.

I still stare at it sometimes, tearing frantically through dusty shelves and stacked cupboards to find it, to hold it up too close to my face so that it almost touches my nose, so that I sometimes leave a nose print on it. I stare at it and stare at it.

It is the only true picture of myself that I have.

That is what that picture is all about.

And also the end. The picture is truly the end.

Sometimes I just feel so heavy.

I am twenty-nine.

My name is Anna Woods.

I am on the fifty-ninth hour of my demoralizing nicotine withdrawal.

And there are all of these things I've done (I can't deny them), all of these cities I've seen and lived in and passed through and slowly deciphered one by one, and all of these pores I've irrevocably opened, and all of these men I've experienced, and all of these jobs I've held, and all of these apartments and rooms I've rented, and all of these products I've used, and all of this food I've consumed, and all of these movies and books and CDs I've devoured, and all of these hairs I've bleached, and all of these sexual acts I've committed like goddamn crimes, and I just feel so heavy, *so goddamn weighed down by it all.*

I sold, discarded, and gave away almost everything I owned, including the Dubble Bubble cat, but I'm still, *still* not getting any lighter—I can still feel all of this *past*, all of this fucking *experience,* and it weighs a goddamn ton. It just weighs so goddamn much. I am only twenty-nine, but sometimes I wonder, I am forced now to wonder: Just how much more can I stand?

No really, I'm asking.

I'm so tired. Tired of being in a city that does not understand what language I'm speaking, or rather of not understanding theirs. These last five weeks have been so tiring, so stressful, so demanding, so lacking in purpose—other than waiting for Jack, that is.

So much of this was forgotten. And remembering it now, I have to wonder why I've pinned so many of my hopes on this one...well, this one asshole really. There are plenty of other men in my past, more than enough other options to choose from. In fact, I'm starting to realize that I have altogether too many options, that I have been, perhaps, more prolific than most, maybe even more prolific than necessary.

There is the one who taught me how to boil an egg. (Quite recently actually.)

There is the one who sold vacuum cleaners.

There is the one who kissed Allen Ginsburg.

There is the one who was almost a famous drummer.

There is the one who made me watch his 'died-this-year' awards show tapes.

There is the one who's now on the evening news. (Surprisingly enough as a newscaster and not a criminal, and who pisses me off because whenever I see him, while searching for a rehash of the day's events, I am instantly reminded of not only his curiously soft breasts, but also of just how low I am willing to go.)

There is the one who told me my hair was too weird.

There is the one who told me my hair was too cool.

There is the one who tasted like milk.

There is the one who probably isn't still straight. (More than one?)

There is the one who worshiped Phil Collins.

There is the Londoner.

There is the Frenchman.

And there are plenty of others as well, plenty that I don't even remember, will not remember. Or at least pretend not to remember.

But I will say this: there haven't been any hockey fans. Beyond the Londoner, there isn't a single hockey fanatic in the bunch, and this in itself is something of an accomplishment.

Yet I don't feel accomplished.

They haunt me, these men. Not just Jack, but all of these past lovers with their varying shapes and sizes, their differing degrees of importance, shamefulness, pleasure, memorability. They haunt me.

Because I believed in each and every one.

Because each and every one was an attempt to stop going it alone, to find *the one*.

Because each and every one has turned out to be a failure, so many fucking failures.

Because suddenly, lately, recently, I want less. Give me a half-kilo of no more, please. In fact, just give me *the one*. I think I'm ready for the one.

But I can hear your answer. I already know your answer: *Sorry, ma'am, that item is no longer available. That will definitely be something we'll have to place on back order.*

So I look back through the catalog at all the men I've believed in—and that part of me still does believe in—and I wonder which one it is, which one will come back for me. And it always comes back to Jack. I always end up at Jack. Because I may believe in each and every one of them, but unfortunately I believe in Him the most.

Life resumed. There was a graduation. There was a boyfriend. There was a first job, a career change, a second job, then no more boyfriend. I was suddenly twenty-nine. Things were different. Everything felt so different, so *not* twenty-two-years-old. I thought about Him occasionally. I toyed with the idea of finding Him—just for a laugh. But such a thing was impossible. Even then.

I admit I clung to my photograph at times. But only on the melancholy days. There were all sorts of days in between—hopeful days, almost-happy days, years of don't-even-notice-'em days, busy days, life days. And then six and a half years after I'd closed the door on His face, I logged onto the Flin Flon website and found a message from Him.

Once again, I'd been found.

It was Halloween. Mischief-makers whooped on the streets outside. My Dubble Bubble cat slept peacefully in her favorite chair, oblivious to my imminent betrayal.

I read the message over and over and over again. Each and every word slipped perfectly over my skin. They fit. They all fit. They fit me.

It read: *Looking for a girl named Anna who grew up in Flin Flon then studied Social Work in Toronto.* (This is amazingly true!) *She loves to cut a rug. I'd love to say hello.*

The message was posted Oct. 3rd. There was no name attached. There was only an indecipherable e-mail address: popfan@yabla.net.

I thought it immediately. I thought it straightaway. I thought Jack. It's that crazy Yankee mutherfucker Jack.

And without thinking—because if I'd actually been thinking, I might have had a friend respond to the message or I might not have responded to it at all or I might have made up a new e-mail address that didn't involve my full name, because really, when you think about it, who knows which of my men might have posted such a message, never mind to what end—without thinking, I fired off a reply.

I wrote: *Hello.*

Then I checked my e-mail every hour on the hour for what turned out to be four excruciatingly long days, during which—with equal certainty—I knew it was Him and knew it was not Him, wanted it to be Him and did not want it to be Him.

But who else? Who else could it possibly be?

Course there've been so many others, haven't there? I'll take a plate-full of decidedly less, please. I'll just take the one now, thank you very much.

Too late, ma'am. It's too goddamn late.

Four nerve-wracking days after I'd hastily and perhaps foolishly sent my e-mail reply, between the hours of ten and eleven a.m. when I had almost given up hope (which again is quintessential Jack and I), the e-mail arrived.

It began: *Cue drum roll...this is your long-lost American pal Jack here...*

I leaned back from my laptop. I shook my head. I saw goose bumps on my arms. Mutherfucking Jack, I thought. I knew it. Because who else would track me down? Because who else was anywhere near as unpredictable and exciting as Jack? Because who else could make me feel this way?

And the header on the e-mail told me His last name was Hammer—*Jack Hammer!*

I began to laugh. I felt wild, reckless, instantly alive again, instantly so high. I was *found!*

Jack Hammer!

I laughed and laughed and laughed. I lifted up the Dubble Bubble cat and spun her around until she woke up enough to firmly bite my hands. Then I put her down. But I couldn't stop laughing. I laughed and laughed and laughed.

This is definitely one of my high points. This is a totally euphoric high point.

We were hesitant to begin. We were unsure. We were casual.

Shall we correspond?

Would you like to correspond?

I don't know. Would you?

Oh what the hell, let's correspond.

It became regular. It became every few days. It became the highlight of my week. It became a reason to go on.

Still, it took two months before the subject of marital status was broached. He couched the question in a jokey, form-like questionnaire. I filled it out, sent a similar one back to Him. Breathless anticipation until the answers arrived: single. Both of us single.

We started to argue and agree and compliment each other and tease each other.

We played nice. We played coy. We did not play sexy. (Which is strange considering that that's almost wholly how I remember our relationship: one big, magical, power-shifting fuck-fest.)

We wrote about movies and books and TV and music and our lives. Although when you think about it—or after you see *Fight Club*—perhaps these amusements were our lives.

We gave each other what is commonly known as information about ourselves as people.

We wrote like old friends.

We did not suggest sex or meeting or even the details of our past, beyond some vague apologies on His part—long overdue I might add.

We started to fall in love again. Or at least I did. Though I said nothing, wrote nothing. Though we never declared love even back then, even after month upon month of sex and drink and arguments, stumbling towards and away from each other as everything began to feel *so much more significant* than it ever had before.

I wanted to send Him three-page-long e-mails outlining the fact that we *must* be together. I laughed giddily (though never to Him) over the impossibility, the romantic impossibility of our reconnection *after all these years*. I wanted to board the next plane to Seattle. I wanted to buy a Jeep and drive the whole way there without stopping for so much as a bathroom break or a box of Timbits.

But I said nothing. I wrote nothing. I drove nowhere. I told Him my last name and how my family was and what I did for a living and for so-called fun. He told me about life on the west coast and how His family was and about His job (lucrative software testing, but only until His photography career took off) and what He did for so-called fun (as if anything could be more fun than our e-mails), which turned out to be a staggering variety of recreational drugs.

And then five months later, while He was obsessing over *Fight Club* again and just as I was on the verge of doing it myself, on April 1ˢᵗ, He wrote: *Let's totally do that and meet.* And I couldn't help but wonder if it was an April Fool's Day joke, though He assured me that it was not. (Although lately I'm not so sure He was telling the truth.)

I lived in Toronto with my Dubble Bubble cat. And I didn't give a shit about *Fight Club* or pop culture or that my near-perfect wardrobe was somehow *wrong*, but I did give a shit about Jack. I gave a big shit about Jack fucking Hammer.

And I laughed, 'cause this was a few months ago and I was thrilled that He'd finally proposed the meet and it all seemed like a lark back then (though not a joke), and I wrote: *Okay dude.*

Somewhere kinda cut off, He wrote. *Somewhere remote but not too remote. My cousin went to Budapest recently. What about Budapest?*

I can be there end of May.

Deal.

Hanging on the wall of this room in Budapest, there is a print of a woman kneeling. It is dim. It is mostly composed of brown and mustard hues. It makes me squint. I cannot tell why this woman is kneeling, nor what she is doing as she kneels, though there is an object in her hands which could be a handkerchief, or a balled-up letter, or a bundle of wool, or any number of whitish, smallish, vague-ish objects.

This picture should depress me—I equate this color scheme with dank pits and unspeakable messes—but it does not. There is a warmth in it that even I cannot deny.

Today, on the morning of June 20th, my third day of withdrawal, while lying here in this stinking chair-bed in Budapest, Hungary listening compulsively to the Radiohead *Amnesiac* CD on my Discman, I have a vision. It is during that song about doors—track three?—the one that scares me, because the sound travels in and out of my headphones from one side to the other with an alarmingly flat intensity. Yes, I think it is track three.

And as Thom Yorke and the boys articulate everything that I've never been able to articulate (though I hope to someday), I glance up at the print, this print that I now know so well, and in the print, I see the woman (impossibly) rise from her knees. The painted woman rises jerkily to the music, as though she is a stop-motion figure slowed way down.

I blink.

And she does it again. With the music. As it travels from one ear to the other, she jerks up.

Jerk, jerk, jerk.

I close my eyes and listen to the frightening song. Thom Yorke intones his compelling though repetitive thoughts about doors directly into my ears. And I keep my eyes closed as I do not wish to see this two-dimensional woman get up—*kneel, kneel, kneel.*

And when I look up again, she is as she has been: crouched and indecipherable and kneeling. And I am calmed. In spite of the fact that I am now hallucinating on a regular basis—the ceiling, the door handle, the woman—I feel remarkably calm. Though the frequency of my heart palpitations does seem to be increasing rather than decreasing.

I am on the sixty-third hour of my hallucinatory withdrawal from nicotine. No point in smoking now, I think as my heart twitches erratically. No point at all now that I'm so close to the magic seventy-two-hour mark.

The painted woman kneels. I diligently watch her, hold her there with my eyes as I slip in and out of consciousness.

Still, I wouldn't mind a quick drag.

I can't wait to see you, He wrote.

And the worst part is that, once again, I totally believed Him.

My roots are truly mesmerizing. I find myself getting up to check them out in the mirror. I find myself actually able to get up out of this Hungarian chair-bed for this purpose. For my unrelenting roots.

Whether or not to bleach my hair in Eastern—or is it Central?—Europe is now a question of the utmost importance.

I stare into the spotted bathroom mirror.

It strikes me as high-risk at best—I have seen very little correct blonde hair in Budapest—but look at these roots. Just look at them. It occurs to me that I may never come to a decision on this front, that I might even be finding this conundrum perversely enjoyable. Perhaps because insoluble?

They are drilling the pavement in the courtyard of this Hungarian apartment building and it is actually shaking the floor of my room. That is the instability of the structure I'm currently inhabiting—which means my roof-caving-in anxiety is not as unlikely as one might hope.

The pipes are rattling.

I glance up at the crack in the ceiling expectantly.

Nothing happens.

I shuffle over to my window, which looks out onto an inexplicable gray hollow of vertical space. It was called a sub-courtyard in the brochure, but it's really just a dark airshaft in the corner of the building, boxed in on all sides by lavatories, with at least one exception—my room. All day and night, I listen to the sounds of human excretion.

There must have been a reason for this construction. What explanation could there be for this particular construction?

But I don't have a clue.

I am shaking.

The floor is shaking.

A toilet flush echoes.

So fucking appropriate, I think. So goddamn apropos.

The Frenchman skitters across my mind.

I am on the sixty-sixth hour of my profane withdrawal from nicotine and I don't think I liked Jack this much even when we were together. Or did I? I'm afraid I can't be sure. I used to call Him Mr. Right Now. But I can't seem to remember whether I was trying to get a reaction or if I knew He was a temp.

Now He is Mr. Right. Despite my feeble denials, this is how I think of Him. Maybe it's how I have always thought of Him. Maybe that is the heart of the problem.

(Meanwhile His real name is Jack Hammer. Which is less likely?)

I pull out my Discman and turn on Radiohead's new album. I cannot stop listening to the new Radiohead album. I listen to it over and over and over again. I cannot understand a fucking word that Thom Yorke is saying half the time. What the fuck is he talking about anyway? But maybe I do not need the words. I hear anger. I hear pain. Venomous hurt. This much I know. This much I understand: *He is very upset.*

There is a brief, but deep inhalation at the beginning of track four. I hit the Track Back button over and over and over again. I breathe with him. Thom Yorke and I breathe together. Over and over and over. Until I am lightheaded and can feel it in my chest.

Siiiiiiip...

Siiiiiiip...

Siiiiiiip...

I am addicted to the sound of Thom Yorke's breath.

I track back.

I track back.

I track back.

I can't seem to stop tracking back—this constant addiction.

I quit smoking, He wrote me a week ago. *I broke free and it was a snap.*

Me too, I typed in reply, taking a long and casual haul off of my Hungarian cigarette.

It's the unwavering clarity of the issue that really kills me. If you have even *one* cigarette, you are back at the beginning. Just one and you are a smoker again. There is no gray area, no mercy, no leniency.

Cigarette, cigarette, cigarette...

My name is Anna Woods.

I am twenty-nine.

And I wonder: Has anyone ever had a heart attack going cold turkey?

And I wonder: Is your chest *supposed* to twitch like this?

And I wonder: Shouldn't I be under some form of medical supervision?

I am almost on the sixty-seventh hour of my feverish nicotine withdrawal, and I am still lying in an odious chair-bed in Budapest, Hungary watching my chest pop in and out. I have been in this town for more than five weeks. I have already fucked a man here. This is not impressive. I am so not impressed. (Though in my defense, he was French. And in my further defense, months of stripped-down European pleasure and leisure with Jack motherfucking Hammer had just been substantially delayed.)

This constant sound of pissing and shitting and farting. Must everyone relieve themselves within earshot? I am not relieved. I assure you that I am not relieved.

Strip away the bullshit, they said. Bullshit is ba-aad.

And Jack wrote: *We need to do that. That is totally the kind of thing we should do.*

But I don't see anyone else in here under this cracked, triple-D-cup corporate ceiling.

I am suddenly furious.

So typical of men to incite and then run away when their support is most required—though for the record, I don't even believe in women's issues per se. What I do believe, and this quite strongly, is that I don't want to be an idiot. This much I know. And if I am an idiot—which appears to be the case—I sure as hell don't want to be as aware of it as I currently am, lying here alone and stood up and perhaps mentally unhinged in Budapest fucking Hungary.

It is still almost the sixty-seventh hour of my feverish nicotine withdrawal. I still don't have a room with a TV.

Now what, I wonder. Now what the hell am I supposed to do? But there is no one else here to ask.

I am really quite tired. I am really quite, quite, *quite* exhausted by this obsessive rehashing of Jack. Of the Frenchman. Of the Londoner. Of all of my unconscionable men. I cannot stop thinking about all of these men. Do they ever, do you think, think about me? But why would they? And why do I care?

It's just that it feels like they leave themselves with me, like they leave little bits, like they're never really gone. Yet I give nothing to them. They never seem to take anything of me when they go and I just feel so goddamn heavy right now. I just feel so goddamn weighed down.

Maybe just one drag. Do you think one drag would hurt? What the fuck do I care if I smoke in front of Him. Just started again I could say. And now it would be the truth. I just started again, I could say, and maybe even offer up a little cough as evidence.

(He probably won't show up anyhow.)

Breathe in.

Breathe out.

Breathe.

This cannot be good for my heart. I am quite certain that I am doing permanent damage to my heart.

I track back.

I track back.

I track back.

FUCK YOU JACK! FUCK YOU!

Do I seriously think it will be possible to sit across the table from Him after all these years—this maybe love of my life whom I've never been able to forget and who is so wrapped up in cheap rye and cigarettes and sweat and dancing and filth and debauchery that to see Him clean and sober would be startling and most likely an enormous turn-off—do I really think I'll just sit there and *not* smoke?

It is hour sixty-eight of my unbearable nicotine withdrawal and I have just now made an important decision: I simply must smoke. It is obvious that I am dependent, perhaps irrevocably dependent on nicotine and this particularly low moment in my life is probably not the ideal time to strive for independence. I will tell Him the truth when I see Him. Or I will tell Him more lies. Or whatever.

The bottom line is that I must appease the monkey.

And while I'm up, I better check my e-mail too. I have not checked my e-mail in days. There may be a message from Him. He may have cancelled (again) or professed His love (unprecedented) or there may be a new movie out or something.

Something.

It's the only way to reach me after all. And someone may need me, someone may no longer be *all right*. Someone other than myself, that is. I simply *cannot* continue to just lie here: unmoving, unreached, unwell.

I stagger into my tiny Budapestian shower to clean off three days of inactive, sweating, trembling fuzz. The shower wand sprays everywhere, though I really, to be quite honest, do not care. Admittedly I have more than a mild case of the shakes, but it's quite impossible to wash, condition and protein-treat your hair, shave your armpits and legs, wash your ears and the rest of your limp body with one hand always clutching this seashell-pink-colored shower wand, and not get water just everywhere. It's not as though the shower curtain even reaches the bottom of this stall. It's not as though the mess I am making is *entirely* my fault.

Get thee to a pack of cigarettes, my brain mutters as the water sprays just everywhere. Get thee.

I feel so much better.

Standing in front of my moisture-studded mirror clad in a black crew neck and a heavy (excessive?) layer of eyeliner and blush, I can't help but feel better. Perhaps I don't even need a cigarette. I've already reached hour sixty-nine after all.

No, no, I really ought to smoke. It really is the real me. In fact I must. I simply must smoke.

Surveying the room, I feel terribly uneasy. It's been so long since I last left it.

I think: My things will be stolen when I go. (Though really, what do I have that anyone would want?)

I think: My ceiling will collapse when I leave. (Though really, why would I want to be present for that?)

I think: It is obvious that I am *not okay*. (No arguments leap to mind.)

For at least the fourth time, I open my purse and check that my wallet and passport are inside. I am comforted by the presence of these official documents, these identifying papers.

I turn the light out. (Why is my light on in the middle of the day?) I close the door and with a shaky hand, I lock it. I am jittery, but determined. I stand frozen for a moment in the hallway, then wonder if I have locked my packsack.

Did I lock my packsack?

I cannot say with certainty that I did, so I unlock my door, cross the room, open the cupboard, and check the bag. It is locked.

The air in here is foul, I think. The air in here is old. I must get out. I simply must. I turn back to the door and exit again, locking it behind me. I have got to get out of here. I'm going goddamn crazy in here.

My name is Anna Woods.

I am twenty-nine.

I am on my way to buy a desperately needed pack of cigarettes.

I am on the sixty-ninth—and surely the final—hour of my catastrophic nicotine withdrawal.

In just a few moments an unleashed husky will barrel past me on the sidewalk.

In just a few moments that husky will begin to howl.

In just a few moments I will bump into the TESL wanker.

Apparently, the dude's real name is Ian.

PART TWO

After The Dog

"**C**'mon," I finally say that afternoon, the both of us standing just outside the supermarket, the one with absolutely no super qualities about it whatsoever except maybe that it's super-slow and the knickers are quite reasonably priced. Ian is still shaking my hand—shaking, shaking, shaking—so I twist mine and begin to pull him along towards the cigarette shop. "I'm seriously fucking dying for a cigarette."

"Fancy one?" he says in what sounds, at that point, like a foreign language.

Once my brain interprets the words, I stop. He is fumbling in his pocket with his free hand.

"Oh my god," I whimper, while he hands me a cigarette and simultaneously searches himself for a lighter. "I...I haven't smoked in over two days."

"You're joking," he says, then pauses, lighter in hand, eyes as devilish as his skinny body. "Maybe I shouldn't light this for you then."

"Ha!" I say, but it comes out threatening-like. My focus is only on the blue plastic torch in his hand. "Very fucking funny." (I might still be a bit testy from the howling husky incident.)

Ian's thumb rolls smoothly along the silver wheel, then presses down tightly on the black plastic tab. I notice his fingers are long and lean like the rest of his body. I lean in and aim the end of the cigarette towards the flame, but I'm shaky, so it takes a minute or two before I can connect. I feel a pang of guilt—*don't do it!*—just as the end begins to glow. I inhale deeply, close my eyes and do a body-slump against some grimy shop window.

"Oh yeah," I sigh, already dizzy. "Oh. Yeah."

"Why don't we get together then," Ian suggests, quite reasonably really considering the candour of our initial meeting.

But I am so dizzy and guilty/pleased about my nicotine rush, I barely hear him. "What brand are these?" I ask, squinting at the filter, my body weaving and faint with the blessed rush of nicotine.

"Friday," he continues.

"Yeah, sure," I mumble. "This is a good brand."

"Philip Morris. Super Lights."

"*Super* Lights," I repeat with, I admit, over-the-top enthusiasm.

"Do you know where Darshan Café is?"

I nod.

"Friday then."

"Yeah, sure," I say, but really I'm just thinking about how fucking great the Super Light is, and also how that damn dog is still howling around inside my head, and about those cheap knickers being sold in the grocery store, and where I might get my roots done, and how great it feels to be out from underneath my cracked and big-brassiered and internationally-recognisable corporate ceiling, and whether or not there will be an e-mail from Jack confirming that the two of us will finally meet again *after all these years.*

(In no less than two days!)

Which there is. An e-mail from Jack, that is. It is entitled *West Coast Catastrophe.*

I start to giggle. Sitting at station seven in Budapest Bytes a month after receipt of the first message from Jack which informed me of His initial 'unexpected, unavoidable delay' and mere moments after bumping into first the dog, and then Ian, and then a cigarette on the hot June streets outside, I laugh and laugh and laugh. But I'm pretty sure I don't convince anyone around me that there's anything funny. The perspiring girl beside me even shifts her chair a little farther away.

It is June 20th.

I am almost thirty, and I laugh and laugh and laugh. I stare at the print of that one message over and over and over again until my two hundred *forints* and thirty minutes are up.

Jack wrote: *You won't believe this.*

Jack wrote: *I had to cancel my flight.*

Jack wrote: *I know that a second time is so not forgivable.*

He did not need to write: *Ba-dump-bump.*

When I walk away from that message (which in so many ways was to be expected. I mean it's just so typical, isn't it?) and get back to my room, the first thing I do is pick up the gift, His gift, His stupid fucking corny sentimental crap-wrapped gift, and hurl it against the imminent structural disaster of my ceiling.

MUTHERFUCKER!

It makes a thunk but does not, as I was hoping, hit me on the way down. I imagine that the crack in the ceiling worsens, but it probably doesn't. I sit down at my tiny table and unwrap my new packet of Philip Morris *Super* Lights. These *are* super, I think. In fact these may be the only super aspect of my life at this particularly low (lowest?) moment. And as I slowly and methodically and deliberately

----

chain-smoke all twenty cigarettes, I marvel at the gall of anyone—never mind myself—the gall of anyone actually trying to give the things up.

When I am finished the pack, I get up and stumble back to the dingy and cramped smoke shop for a super-fresh pack of whatever they hand me.

I think: I am defeat.

I think: I am *so* defeated.

I think: I am walking, talking, smoking defeat.

A few hours later, feeling sick—you could barbecue a cutlet on my tongue—and sickening, I remember.

Ian. Darshan Café. Friday.

And after being so ruthlessly stood up myself—not only once but twice and in a foreign fucking country by some asshole from my past named Jack Hammer, whom I thought was Mr. Right, but who is just so clearly Mr. Wrong—I couldn't stand someone else up, could I?

No. No, I didn't think I could.

And why not really? Why not give this 'TESL wanker', this Ian a shot? He could be the one. I could believe in him, couldn't I? At least he was in the same goddamn city.

But really, if I'm being honest, these are fleeting thoughts. Mostly I just think about what a mutherfucker Jack is. And whether or not my mouth could stand another Philip Morris *Super* Light. And why that dog is still howling around deep inside my head—just what in the hell is that dog trying to tell me anyway?

Let's get one thing straight: Ian was never part of the plan.

In fact, almost immediately after our voracious make-out session in the middle of the dance floor at Old Man's Pub—a spectacle whose main purpose had been to repel the hockey-loving, Jeep-driving Londoner, although it must also be admitted that I thoroughly enjoyed myself—almost immediately thereafter I looked forward to the moment when I might forget the 'TESL wanker's' devilishly skinny body *and* my unforgivable behaviour that drunken evening altogether. So running into him on the street these few weeks later, while helpful in an emergency-nicotine-replenishment sense, was rather unfortunate in a forgetting-appalling-behaviour sense.

But to my delight, Ian the TESL wanker turns out to be something of a find once I finally pay attention to him, which I do end up doing that Friday at Darshan Café, not able as it turns out—though I really wasn't sure until the last minute—not able to stand him up as I had just been so horribly stood up by that asshole Jack. Again, I might add. Stood up in a foreign fucking land *again*, and for the second time, so, you know, points for consistency and all that.

My first impression of Ian, because despite random street-smoking encounter and hearty make-out session this is the first time I've really *looked* at him, my first impression is that he is a typical, pasty Brit. Or at least my idea of a typical, pasty Brit, which, it must be noted, has been heavily influenced by the infectious-but-melancholy English pop music scene.

Tall, thin, unearthly pale skin under a ragged mass of straggly hair, big nose. Kinda rock-star. Kinda Richard Ashcroft—hot in a not typically hot kinda way. Which is *totally* my type. (Or maybe I'm just not feeling particularly picky at that admittedly low moment in my life. Who can say for sure?)

Familiar too. Something familiar about him. And I *really* like that. Because I've recently been toying with the idea of homesickness. (Though I really can't go home. Not without a love story. And certainly not with the current story which, so far, seems to be the antithesis of a love story.)

"We owe it all to the Londoner," I say to Ian that first night over pints of Tuborg.

"Which Londoner?"

"My friend. The Canadian who was with me at Old Man's."

"I don't follow."

"Not London, England. London, Ontario." I say it as though I am revealing a clever trick. "I kissed you because I wasn't attracted to him."

Ian blinks. "I see," he says, but I don't think he does.

I laugh. I think I'm being charming. I think this is acceptable conversation. It is possible that despite resumption of smoking habit, I still may not be all right. "He called you the 'TESL wanker' for the rest of his visit," I continue. "I had to go along with it, 'cause he was surprisingly cool about the whole thing."

There is no discernible expression on Ian's face. "I appreciate your honesty," he finally says.

I shrug. I have no idea if he's being sarcastic. This man is a mystery to me. Completely new. And indecipherable. Though not wholly unfamiliar.

(About all I can say for myself at this point is that at least I don't mention Jack. At least I don't say we also owe that asshole Jack, that tonight is the night I was supposed to be reunited with Him again after all these years. *June 22nd*, He wrote a month ago. *I promise.* Though He is quite clearly MIA. He is quite clearly breaking yet another promise.)

Ian and I smoke.

Ian and I talk.

Ian and I drink four pints each.

He tells me he loves my accent. He tells me he can't stop listening to the new Radiohead album. He tells me he loves teaching English abroad and also—and perhaps more importantly from my standpoint—that his waist is a mere twenty-nine inches in circumference.

I tell Ian I love his accent. I tell him I can't stop listening to *Pyramid Song*. I tell him I love speaking

English abroad and also that I love men with twenty-nine-inch waists.

Ian laughs and touches my hand. He passes me a Philip Morris *Super* Light. He orders us another round.

"You look just like a rock star," I say to him later that night as he exposes his absurdly skinny chest. "Or maybe a junkie."

I search his arms for track marks. He lets himself be searched. We sit together on his brown loveseat. Ian passes me a Philip Morris *Super* Light. I stare at his eyes. I cannot figure out what colour his eyes are. Some sort of greenish-brown.

Outside the flat, someone or something is systematically setting off one car alarm after another as he or she or it progresses slowly down the street. Just as one stops, another begins. Madness, I think. Total madness.

"You look gorgeous," Ian whispers in my ear. "Totally gorgeous."

What language is he speaking, I wonder just before my brain interprets the words. (Even with my full concentrative powers, I think that, in the beginning at least, I am only grasping about sixty per cent of his intent.)

I smile.

He smiles.

A new car alarm begins to drone outside, a honking bass line.

Hazel, I think. Is that the colour? I take a drag and pass the cigarette back to him. No, I don't think it's hazel at all. I seem to be losing my grasp on the English language. Even the simplest of words seems difficult to recall in the midst of all of this foreignness.

He kisses me.

I kiss him back.

But this is the night that Jack and I were to be reunited, and I can't seem to forget that fact for more than a few seconds. So I give up trying.

"I have to go."

"Stay."

"I have to go."

"You don't."

I search for a turn-off. "I'm almost thirty."

"You don't look a day over twenty-nine."

I smile. "I have to get up early. I'm getting my hair done in the morning."

"Are you?" He smiles devilishly. "But your hair is gorgeous."

I think: I definitely want to sleep with this man. I say: "I didn't realise you Brits were so charming."

"Never realised you Canadians were so sexy."

I think: Jack was supposed to say these things to me tonight. Jack was supposed to be here. I stand up. "I'm going."

Ian stares up at me from the loveseat. He says: "When can I see you again?"

I smile coyly and pretend to consider the question, but all I'm really thinking is: Take that, Jack. Take that.

The salon is dead, as in there is no one else in the salon. This is never a good sign. I feel sick. I feel hours away from mere queasiness. I feel hungover as hell. The receptionist stares at me. I stare at the receptionist. Her hair resembles fake wood panelling, faux wood grain and all.

I think: Run! Run for your life!

Then I catch a glimpse of myself in the mirror: roots. Almost-seven-week-long roots.

I should have planned this better. I should never have touched up my hair for my final week of farewell parties. I should have seen Marla the day, perhaps the very hour before I left Toronto. I should have bought Marla and her North American expertise a one-way ticket to Budapest. I should have at least made some kind of half-assed plan—or was this it?

Smiling at the receptionist, I point at my roots and then at her giant appointment book.

She says something in Hungarian.

I shake my head. "I don't understand."

Her eyes twinkle. She ushers me into a chair so quickly that I feel it entirely possible I might vomit.

The receptionist confers with the only other two people in the room: a middle-aged woman sporting a stupendous bouffant and a back-combed girl with jet black hair and a wad of pastel pink chewing gum in her mouth. The exact hue of my dear cat's nose, I think. The poor Dubble Bubble cat whom I so callously abandoned for that asshole Jack Hammer. This thought, of course, incites an anxious stomach churn of unadulterated guilt.

All three of the ladies turn to glance at me and then continue on with their huddle. I wonder which of them will do the honours, but I don't even bother making a preference. There doesn't seem to be much point in it.

I skim my mini-phrasebook, looking for applicable Hungarian words, but it turns out to be of no help at all. It turns out the Hungarian phrasebook lacks subtlety: words like *highlights* and *minimal damage* and *low-lift blonde* are not contained in this mini-book.

Finally the eighteen-year-old gum chewer saunters over to me with the over-sized colour book in hand. She opens it with a flourish, then lightly skims my hair and my screeching headache with her fingertips. I wince. I pass her a small card. Written on it is Marla's personalised colour-stripping formula, the entire reason for my coming to this particular salon in the first place, as it is the only one I could find that also used Goldwell products. And I figure, how hard can it be? Once they have the formula, all they have to do is apply, right? How difficult can the application be?

The girl stares at the card, confused. The girl snaps her gum thoughtfully. The girl passes the card to the woman with the grey bouffant. Together they frown at it. I of course have it memorised, just in case. I gesture to the two women. I take the card. I point at each item on the card and then at the corresponding colour swatch in the colour book. The two women nod their heads vigorously. They take the colour book away. They carry the card to the mixing station. I watch as they both hesitate and then simultaneously pull down colour tubes. I watch as they pour indiscriminate amounts into a small plastic dish.

This is a mistake, I think. *Run!* But my stomach is churning. My head is pounding. I am quite incapable of flight.

The girl carries the plastic dish containing some semblance of my formula over to me. She mixes it with a black plastic paintbrush. It makes a decisive, clicking sound against the edge of the dish. She parts my hair roughly.

We stare at each other for a moment.

She snaps her gum.

I look away and close my eyes.

Oh no, I think as the first sting of high—perhaps the highest?—volume bleach burns my scalp. *Oh no.*

I open my eyes. I watch the eighteen-year-old work: blue bleach slapped willy-nilly onto my head. The colour bears absolutely no resemblance to the goop Marla used to apply so lovingly and so seemingly long ago. The girl snaps her chewing gum with passion. She does not seem to recognise the demarcation line that separates natural, dark roots from previously-treated hair.

This is an irrevocable mistake, I think, even as it is happening. But there seems to be no choice. What else can I do?

I close my eyes again, try to think of something other than my prickling scalp, my (practically) steaming hair. I recall the events of the previous evening. I recall Ian, Ian's delightful accent, Ian's soft lips.

"When can I see you again then?" he asked as I was leaving. "What are you up to on Sunday?"

The girl roughly tilts my neck forward, which allows me to surreptitiously check my watch so that I might time the bleach, the stinging, draining, colour-stripping bleach that is being slapped so unceremoniously onto my head.

This is so not low-lift blonde.

This is so not subtle.

This is so not going to turn out okay.

Run. *Run!*

But where to? Where the hell would I go?

I stay. I think about Ian. I think about how Ian told me I was gorgeous. Did Jack ever tell me such a thing? I can't recall Him ever saying such a thing. But Ian did. I was starting to like this Ian.

(Though I have to wonder, if I am being truly honest, I wonder if it might not be the catastrophe with Jack that is making Ian so appealingly seductive in the first place. But then who cares, really. Who gives a good goddamn about reasons so long as somebody wants me. So long as some kind of love story takes place here.)

The eighteen-year-old behind me blows a giant bubble over my prickling and pounding head. When it pops, it leaves a small patch of pastel pink on her nose.

This is a terrible mistake, I think, as the entirety of my scalp begins to itch unbearably. The girl yanks a plastic bag over my head. I follow her in the mirror as she walks away from me wearing a mischievous smile.

Thirty minutes later, standing behind me and still snapping the same (as far as I can tell) wad of pink bubble gum, the eighteen-year-old makes a cutting motion with

----

her fingers. She raises her brows into an international question.

I stare at her reflection. I stare at her back-combed hair. I stare at her peppy pink chewing gum. I recall how ruthlessly and recently and, above all, *unnecessarily* she had slathered the remainder of the bastardised version of Marla's formula onto my already fragile, already blonde ends. I'd waved my hands frantically, my eyes bulging with the impossibility of communication.

But it had been too late.

I glance at my newly-sizzled hair and shake my head slowly. *"Nem,"* I say, feeling actual grief. *"Nem."*

Nem means no, I think, laughing bitterly at the feminist slogan.

The girl shrugs. The girl uncoils her hairdryer. The girl snaps her gum.

I picture the Frenchman and his outstretched fingers. I see his mouth open, his lips purse. I hear him say *pas de parfait* in his oh-so-French way.

The girl clicks on the hairdryer. The girl blow-dries my hair. I watch as my new hair colour is slowly revealed. I watch as my ends get whiter and whiter and drier and drier. I watch as the ends split, as the ends snap right off. I watch as one of them gets caught in the back-combed girl's gum.

And then I see that the roots aren't even gone. That the roots are lighter, yes, but still golden, hideously golden against the stark white that is now the rest of my hair.

I think: Seriously, *pas de parfait.*

I think: No one will find me gorgeous now.

I think: Enough with this blow-drying.

And I am overcome by a willful sort of homesickness. I miss Marla. I miss her salon. I miss the possibility of natural-looking fake blonde hair. I miss everything, yet nothing *specifically*. When I think about home, I see a vague sort of smudge, like the blur of the world without my eyeglasses.

I wonder if my mini-phrasebook might contain the Hungarian equivalent for protein treatment. But I doubt it. I sincerely doubt it.

My eyes are swollen. I've barely slept. I am standing outside of Ian's apartment building trying to focus on the buzzer board. I have no idea what Ian's buzzer number might be and the names seem strictly Hungarian: *Barkoczy, Kertai, Alkonyi...*

I stare at the board. I can dimly make out my own reflection in the shimmery plastic weather shield. Mostly I see my white, white hair, my golden roots. I step back from the buzzer board and glance at my watch. I was supposed to meet him ten minutes ago, about the time I realised I had no phone number for him, no buzzer code. It had seemed like a sign, like I ought to just turn around and walk away, keep that hair to myself...

There is a vacant lot across the street. I cross over to it. I am careful to avoid the ubiquitous dog shit underfoot. I stare up at Ian's building and recall that he is on the top floor, the fourth floor. There are two open windows on that floor that I can see.

I look around, see no one else on the street. It is Sunday afternoon; the street is dead. I open my mouth. I call out: "Ian!"

The sound bounces back and forth between the grey buildings that flatly line the street.

"Ian!"

I see a mass of dark hair lean out of a window.

"Hiya!" he yells. "I'll be right down."

He disappears before I can respond. I saunter back across the street, touch my hair nervously. Will he find me gorgeous now? Is such a thing even possible?

The thick wooden door opens and there is Ian.

"Thought you might not make it," he says.

I stare at him. The twists and turns of his accent require my full concentration. Finally I say: "I don't know your buzzer." (And already my own accent is beginning to sound clunky—a bawdy bump-n-grind to his gliding sing-song.)

He motions me inside. He doesn't seem to notice my hair, but then we are in a mercifully dark foyer. He kisses me. I kiss him back. I try not to enjoy it too much—as soon as he gets a whiff of the hair, I figure I'll be hitting the bricks.

"It is so good to see you again."

"Yeah?"

He shrugs. "You should have stayed the other night."

"Thank god I didn't. I was in total pain at the salon."

"Ah, the hair. Give us a look then." He pulls me towards the sunlit courtyard in the centre of the building. Normally, I love these inner courtyards—surprises wrapped up in monolithic grey boxes—but I could have done without this particular one at that particular moment.

"It's not good," I say, pulling back a little. "It's not-"

Ian reaches up with his fingers. He touches my hair and smiles. "Gorgeous," he says.

You have got to be kidding.

He leans in to kiss me again.

Eyes closed, I think. Good plan. Keep his eyes closed.

"Fancy a beer before we go out?"

"Definitely."

We ride the tiny elevator up five floors. We walk into Ian's apartment. Ian shuts the door behind me. Ian puts his skinny rock-star arms around my waist and smiles devilishly. He says: "I don't actually have any beer."

I put my arms around his twenty-nine-inch waist. "S'okay. I didn't come up for the refreshments."

Ian touches my hair and whispers in my ear. He says: "Gorgeous."

I think: What language are you speaking?

And then my brain interprets the word.

"When can I see you again?" Ian keeps asking me every morning after, despite the worsening condition of my hair. "When can I see you again?"

Which is goddamn delightful, I have to say. So polite and proper and...unlikely. Has anyone ever asked me this question before? It is so not a North American question. A Canadian man would say: "Uhh...yeah...uh...maybe we should hook up again...or somethin'...or not...Hey, do you think we'll ever fuck?..."

And not only is this a question that no one seems to have asked me before, but it certainly, definitely, positively is not a question that anyone has ever *repeatedly* asked me. It's a goddamn declaration. This is an out-and-out declaration. And I have to admit that this lean and pasty and big-nosed Brit is quite lovely. This lean and pasty and big-nosed Brit may just have a shot.

"When can I see you again," he keeps saying.

And the answer turns out to be all the damn time.

He leads me through Budapest, always touching me, holding my hand or curving his gangly arm around my waist or shoulder. He introduces me to a seemingly inexhaustible selection of Budapest's patios (he calls them beer gardens), pubs, clubs, restaurants—all of them dirt-cheap and well-stocked with international liquor, though each and every one offering what can only be described as the poorest of service.

I have been here for over six weeks now and thought myself to be quite well-oriented, but I find myself constantly lost with him, quite unsure of where I am, where he is taking me, which direction home is. Perhaps it is that he actually pronounces the street names, assembled consonants that bear no resemblance to how they look like they should sound. Or perhaps it is the paths he chooses, paths I've never seen before though they probably all run parallel to the streets I know.

We eat.

We drink.

We screw.

Occasionally I wonder: Where are you taking me? Or: Where the hell are we? Or: How the hell do you keep so slim? But mostly I just follow him. Because he's connecting me to this new world, acting as my guide. Not just showing me the city from the standpoint of a local, but explaining certain customs, and teaching me how to say things in Hungarian, things like *excuse me* and *how much* and *two large beer, please*. I stare at his lips as he says them. I sound them out. I say them shyly and incorrectly, and every day I feel a little less like a tourist, a little less away from home. And Ian doesn't get frustrated when I say the words wrong. He just pats my hand and patiently repeats them, something devilish, something indecipherable constantly lurking behind his eyes, the colour of which I still cannot identify.

He's not so polite in the bedroom. There he leaves bruises on me, new ones appearing each day. On my thigh or my breast, a full set of fingerprints on my upper left arm that just will not fade away. I stare at my new bruises. Maybe my skin just can't get used to being touched again; it's been so long.

"You bruise easily," Ian says.

"I guess I do," I reply, though I've never noticed it before.

That's the other thing. Ian points out all of this stuff I've never noticed before. Because we're different. We're from different worlds and all of our differences are just so bloody fascinating. Which is maybe why he looks so devilish to me, why everything he says carries the ambiguity of a potential second meaning—at least a second meaning, possible a third, maybe even a fourth...

"Just lie back and think of England," Ian jokes.

But the weird part is that I do. And the weirder part is that it turns me on.

I say cookie. He says biscuit.

I say bangs. He says fringe.

I say ass. He says arse. Though I must confess that I occasionally do make him say ass. I love how his accent strains towards arse and how he mocks himself—or maybe me—when he says it. Or perhaps it's just the sibilance that turns me on. All of it turns me on. I am so constantly turned on. But I cannot help thinking, I cannot help but wonder: What happens when we run out of difference? Just what the hell happens then?

But then Ian says 'taking the piss' or some such nonsense, and I forget all about my worries.

Incidentally, Jack, a.k.a. Mr. Wrong, still writes to me. He sends me an e-mail a day. He gives them funny titles like *I'm such an asshole* and *Look at me, I'm a big fat prick.*

But I just hit Delete.

Delete.

Delete.

Delete.

Because what could He possibly say at this point? What could He possibly have to say?

Bloody tosser...

I meet most of Ian's friends on July 1st, Canada Day.

We end up in a drinking den called Vichman's, a grimly lit room consisting of five folding tables, a makeshift bar such as you might find in a North American basement back in the fifties, and a toilet. It has all the ambience and none of the attendance of a small-town social.

I am perched on Ian's knee. That is how packed with people our table is and I cannot remember the last time I sat amongst such a large group, though it was definitely back in Canada. I have not been a member of a group like this since I so cavalierly abandoned my cat, my life, my home back in Canada.

Everyone is in good spirits, or rather copious and cheap spirits are in them. Ian and I kiss almost constantly. The rest of the table pretends not to notice, though whether this is out of a sense of decorum or repulsion, I really could not say.

Every few minutes or so, when the conversation lags—which is often, considering both the levels of intoxication and the cornucopia of nationalities and languages present at this table: Hungarian, British, Canadian, Czech, Romanian, Spanish, god-knows-what-else—someone raises their glass and with a startling verve, yells: "HAPPY CANADA DAY!!!!"

And the whole table laughs, for that is the big joke of the evening: what an unimaginatively named and heretofore unheard-of (except by me obviously) holiday my country has. But everyone smiles wildly, and with the greatest of goodwill raises their glass and takes another big gulp of dodgy, Hungarian, drinking-den beer. And in a weird way, sitting amongst this multicultural group, I feel like I'm home. Or maybe even better than if I were at home.

Earlier I was asked: "It is like American Independence Day, yes?"

"Yes, yes," I'd jovially replied, though it later nagged at me. Canada Day wasn't like Independence Day at all. But then I couldn't imagine how to explain the difference, couldn't be sure I even knew the difference, so I drank some more and snogged Ian some more and I forgot all about it.

A few hours later, staggering down broken cobblestone streets with this international pack of drunken fools—Ian of course leading the way—I attempt to sing *O Canada!* to find that I barely know three lines never mind the correct order. Still, not to be denied my moment (because who will know anyway?), I repeat them over and over and over again.

"...O Canada!...from far and wide...O Canada!...true patriot love...the True North strong and free..."

And then I feel a sharp pang, an almost physical jolt of patriotism for a country whose national anthem (which I realise is also unimaginatively titled) I really just couldn't be bothered to learn. How Canadian, I think, quite pleased with my observation, until I realise that no one here would get the joke. None of these people would get it. And then I feel irritated, because it means that no one here really gets me either.

But then Ian stumbles over to me and throws a slender arm across my shoulders.

"Happy Canada Day," he whispers in his (I think) highbrow accent.

And part of me thinks: What do you mean by that?

But the other part of me is so relieved to finally be part of a love story that I throw my arm around his twenty-nine-inch waist and feel somehow connected to home.

"You're gorgeous," he says.

And I smile. This is, of course, better than home.

This week's messages are entitled:
Please forgive me.

You are so the wind beneath my wings.
I can explain.
You know I can't help it. I'm American.
I thought Canadians were supposed to be nice.
Just tell me you're alive.
I stare at the screen. I tick the adjacent boxes. I click on Delete.

One night, after an endless series of outdoor pints and cigarettes, we buy our way into a dingy underground club.

Ian orders our drinks. I love how old world he is—opening doors, ordering drinks, directly declaring his desire to see me again, assuming that I am the sort of woman who expects to be asked. How different he is, I can't help but think again. Different from the North Americans I know. Different from Jack. Different from me. But recognisable too, still somehow recognisable.

"What's that?" I ask, staring at his drink as he passes me a bottle of beer.

"Vodka and Bomba."

It looks like a short glass of lemonade. "What the hell's a Bomba?"

"Energy drink."

I love how Ian is constantly teaching me stuff. I smile. "Gettin' old."

"Twenty-nine. Same as you, young lady."

"Same as your waist," I purr (ridiculously), slipping an arm around him.

We shuffle over to a pillar. We lean against it. It's too loud to talk, so we stare at the crowd, mostly scantily-clad teenagers—and me almost thirty! And standing there with the decidedly bad music (still a member of the international style council!) pounding through my head, I can't help but think of Jack, how often I'd see Jack leaned back against a post just like this one, in some dark and dingy club just like this one. I used to get such a rush when I'd see Him. And I'm not as angry with Him as I'm supposed to be. I know I'm supposed to be a hell of a lot angrier. But all those nights in those clubs…will anyone ever surpass all those nights we had together?

I feel Ian's hand slip round my waist. He leans down to kiss me. I turn my head up and am delighted when a gush of sweet lemony liquid streams from his mouth into mine.

"Yummy," I giggle. (I have not been this uncontrived in years.)

"Bomba," Ian says devilishly.

"Indeed."

And I admit, I must admit, that this lean and pasty and big-nosed Brit may just be getting to me. He is definitely starting to get to me. And I think, again, still, that there is more to this Ian than meets the eye. There is definitely more to this man than I can see.

But the question is: Is there enough? Is there enough to knock Jack off of all those old dance floors? And why, even here, even now, is that American asshole still in my thoughts?

Have I mentioned I'm almost thirty now? I don't think it'll be so bad. It might even be good—come of age, come into my own, embark upon my sexual peak and all that…

How bad can it be?

No really, I'm asking: How bad do you think it will be?

Eighteen. I can count the days now. Eighteen days until I am thirty.

I stare into Ian's bathroom mirror quite transfixed by my frazzled hair. And I can't help but feel a sense of dread, the same sense of dread I've felt at every birthday, ever since Jack stood me up and ended things between us all those years ago. And I almost laugh out loud at how little has changed. Though surely this birthday will be different. Surely Ian is no Jack, Jack is no Ian. Still, I can't help but compare the two. I am quite sickened by my need to compare the two.

"You're such a Canadian," Ian said to me just a minute ago.

I stare at my naked self in the mirror. Apparently, I am such a Canadian. But I don't see it. I don't see anything at all. Same old face. My hair is a tangled and knotted mess. My roots are lighter, but still golden. I look no different. I am no more Canadian than I ever was. Maybe even less so. Am I less Canadian?

Carefully, almost gingerly, I brush my hair. It's not so bad. Maybe this hair is not so bad after all. I think this even though it's obvious that the whole mess is hopeless. Surely things will change after I turn thirty. Surely I'll feel more independent. Freer. Stronger. More myself. Surely I won't feel so...unsure...

The howling dog awakens inside my head. I can hear the dog howl, but the dog's howling message could not be more unclear. Does the dog agree or disagree? Frankly it's difficult to know.

Somehow I thought it would be Jack with me on this birthday. I thought Jack would arrive to make amends for all those years ago. I thought it would be Jack who would reap the rewards of the beginning of my sexual peak.

But it won't be Him. It will be Ian.

"You're such a Canadian," Ian said to me just a minute ago. "That is such a Canadian thing to do." Ian met a lot of Canadians while teaching English in Japan. Ian thinks he knows all there is to know about Canada.

"Meaning?"

Ian smiled and pointed at the light I'd just turned on. I looked up. I didn't get it.

"It's the middle of the day, Anna."

I shrugged and turned out the light, muttered: "Nothing to do with Canada."

And then Ian recounted some (unlikely) story about how I also left all the lights on inside the flat before we went out the other night. And that this innocent oversight has cultural significance as it indicates "my excessive North American consumerism and blatant disregard for the people of the future."

I glared at him with a quick repugnance rising in my throat. I said: "Don't tell me you just watched *Fight Club*."

Ian frowned.

"Dude, it's your flat," I said, shutting myself in the lav. "Turn off your own damn lights."

And it took a full minute before I even noticed that I'd said flat instead of apartment.

"Leave it," I say, still irritated by how Canadian I am.

But he is already up, rock-star chest exposed, pants hardly even half-undone. He lowers the heavy shutter on his ridiculously over-sized window.

"You and that shutter," I say. "You're obsessed."

"Everyone can see in," he chirps in his accent which is still so noticeable, still so different from my own.

"So what," I reply, thinking there is something British about this behaviour, something so obviously English. "We're having sex in your apartment. Big deal." (It gives me great pleasure to act as though I am not a prude. Ever since *Monsieur Parfait* informed me that all North Americans are Puritans I have made it a personal quest to prove him wrong.) "Talk about being British."

Ian shrugs, though he doesn't return until the giant slats are completely lowered.

We gaze at each other for a moment, perhaps incredulously. Then we resume disrobing. But I can't seem to let it go. It becomes my new mantra, some kind of verbal symbol for Ian and his Englishness. One of the few Ian quirks I can predict, see through.

"Shutter down!" I say every time he pauses sexual activity to lower it. "Shutter down!"

I say it in a clipped voice that imitates his accent—*t*'s as sharp as knives. But Ian just ignores me, inscrutable as ever. (And yet also recognisable somehow.)

Mr. Wrong's messages arrive like clockwork. The titles read:

Are you even reading these?
You're really mad, EH?
It's about my photographs...
A gallery wants to show them.
A gallery is going to show them...
How could I say no?
Anna, please...

I sigh. I tick off all of the adjacent boxes. I hit Delete.

Suddenly I cannot see him. We are all fingers and palms and arms wrapped around each other. We're feet and legs on evening cobblestone. We're macro eyes and thick wet tongues. We're so close it's impossible to see anything. Sometimes when I see the whole of him standing across the room or the bar, I am surprised. I always forget how rock-star he really is.

But the stupidest part is that I have begun to call him Mr. Wright. I call him Mr. Wright now, because that, if you can believe, is his name.

My name is Anna Woods.

In eight days, I will turn thirty.

And twenty-nine days after that, I must leave Budapest.

I am practically shacked up with my new British lover Ian on the Pest side of the river, the appropriately lower side of Budapest, but beyond this I have no purpose. I have a nagging feeling that I may in fact require a purpose. Perhaps I have too much time on my hands now that I have stopped thinking about that asshole Jack Hammer. Well, mostly stopped thinking about Him anyway.

"What can I do here?" I ask Ian after we do a shot of Unicum—which I hate, but which Ian seems to love—at Resti Kocsma. I ask him this because I am feeling vague and purposeless and maybe even a little bored—though I wouldn't say I'm *being* boring exactly—and also because we are waiting on our pints which we ordered at least ten minutes ago and which have yet to arrive. And because I do not know what to talk about now that movies and movie stars are no longer an option, because Ian 'couldn't give a toss about that film crap.'

Just to our left is a two-man guitar/organ band. The décor surrounding us is cute Communism. Ian is staring fixedly at a wall of hammer-and-sickle posters.

"Teach English," he says.

I follow Ian's gaze and think: I do like the Communist aesthetic. And in the same instant I'm aware of the pretension of this thought, the boorish North American tourist behind this thought.

"Very funny," I say, because it's possible that Ian may be mocking my sloppy North American speech patterns.

"It's quite interesting," he says.

I notice our waiter is having a leisurely smoke at the bar while we await our nowhere-to-be-seen pints.

"You learn a lot about your own language by hearing a non-native speaker struggle with it."

"Sounds painful," I say while glaring pointedly at the waiter. "Is that why you left England? A passion for spreading the miracle that is the English language?"

"Nah. Pubs just shut too early."

"They do, don't they? What is it, midnight?"

"Eleven."

"That is awful."

The waiter ignores me.

Ian nods. "Later in Canada?"

"Three in Toronto, but it depends what part of the country you're in."

"Does it?"

"Oh yeah. Drinking age too. It's eighteen in some provinces, nineteen in others."

"Makes perfect sense."

I shrug.

"So if not for the pub hours, why'd you leave Canada then?"

"Oh, you know." I blush. "Vacation."

"Gorgeous vacation. How long have you been here, a month?"

"Two."

Ian whistles.

"One more and I gotta go."

"Do you?" There is an indecipherable expression on his face.

"It's the law. Ninety days." I lean in. "Can you believe our waiter is just standing at the bar smoking?"

Ian passes me a Philip Morris *Super* Light, as though my outrage derives from envy.

"Why do you have to do anything?" he asks.

"I don't know. I just feel like I have no purpose."

"Maybe that is your purpose."

I stare at him, pissed off. I wonder: Is this 'taking the piss?' I glare at our waiter who I see is now stubbing out his cigarette.

"Can't you come right back in once you leave?" Ian asks. "Go to Vienna for a day or so, take in some opera and then come back."

"I guess. I don't know."

We stare at the band for a moment. They are halfway though an instrumental version of *My Way*.

"I'm not that into opera."

"Oh, right. I forgot you're North American."

"What's that supposed to mean?"

He smiles devilishly. "Heathens, the lot of you."

I punch his arm semi-playfully.

He laughs through his nose. It's his I-know-I'm-not-supposed-to-laugh laugh.

The waiter finally arrives with our beer.

"Fancy another shot as well?" Ian asks.

"Why not."

But when we turn back to the waiter, he is already at the bar sparking up a fresh cigarette and is unlikely to return for quite some time.

That night we climb up onto one of the support bases of Erszebet Bridge—the white bridge. It takes some time and calculation and cooperation to accomplish it, but eventually we manage, even though, or maybe because, we are Unicum drunk.

We find a sunken section of concrete about the length and width of a grave. I stare straight down into Ian's greenish-brown eyes while my knees throb against the concrete. Heavy clouds of dust—decades of it, whole regimes of it—surround us, land on us, scurry underneath us, billow up over us, slip inside of us. Cars screech past just a few feet below. We are completely hidden from their view and yet so near.

Later we sit silently with our elbows resting on bent knees. We look across the Danube at the lights still glowing on the opposite bank, on the high and hilly side of the river.

The sun is just beginning to rise.

Ian says: "Did you know that Budapest was once two different cities? Buda and Pest, separated by the Danube."

I nod.

"Remarkable, isn't it? These two cities so near each other and yet refusing to merge?"

"Yeah," I whisper, though I'm not sure it's so hard to believe.

"I love this city," he says, staring across the water at Buda. "A city of bridges."

The castle and Fisherman's Bastion hover spectacularly in the early morning light. Chain Bridge looms to our right, its majestic lions standing patient guard at either end.

And I am surprised to find that I feel the same way. "I love it too," I say, barely recalling the mental chaos of my first month here, quite forgetting that I was ever homesick, almost entirely forgetting an American asshole named Jack Hammer.

Ian says: "I don't want you to leave."

I look at him, but he is still staring across the water.

"If you leave, I want you to come back straightaway."

And I can't help but think again that he is so different: different from the North Americans I know, different from Jack, different from me. But still somehow recognisable. And I don't know how I feel about what he has said, but I am glad that he has said it.

I say nothing. I reach out and squeeze his hand. He squeezes back.

After some hazy amount of time, we jump down from our perch. We walk home exhausted and filthy. It is now undeniably morning. We lean on each other for support as we trudge through the beginning-to-bustle streets.

Back at his flat, we collapse onto his single bed. We are covered in thick bridge dust. We leave marks on the bed sheets. We forget, or are too tired to close the shutter. The sun blares through the window as we sleep the day away.

The next afternoon, I wake up to intensely bruised knees: sizable patches of royal purple. All through the week, we stare at them, watching with fascination as they go from almost-black to deep and then light blue, an angry red, then a sullen pink, and finally a mustard brown which reminds me of the printed woman kneeling in my old, cracked room. Every once in a while, Ian reaches out a hand and with gentle fingers strokes them.

He says nothing. I say nothing. But our eyes glaze over and all I can think is yes. Yes, he may just have enough. It is entirely possible he is enough.

I should have my period by now.

In fact I should have had it a week ago, especially since it generally comes like clockwork, but said clock seems to have been redirected to an alternate time zone. Plus I've been ignoring an uneasiness in my belly for a few days now. Loss of appetite too. Probably just a cold. Though something is definitely wrong when I do not crave a beer.

And I am not craving a beer.

The husky howls through my skull, connecting my ears, holding them onto my head—pesky fucking dog.

I stare at Ian's open window. His window is unbelievably large. It's goddamn bigger than my entire living room wall was in Toronto. Suddenly incensed, I get up from the brown corduroy love seat and stride furiously over to it. It's goddamn bigger than a small car. I lean out to see the street below before a rush of nausea pulls me back in.

Every other apartment block I've seen here faces an almost identical grey slab of apartment block, as though mirrors rather than buildings ran up and down the length of every street. (Or, as was my case, you have the gorgeous option of a lavatory air pocket.) But Ian has a deep vacant lot across the street, so that the view now is of a distant, domed building and a pink, falling-sun sky. They glow together magnificently.

This is the best goddamn view in Budapest, I think, incredibly pissed off.

But it occurs to me that I may be overreacting. It occurs to me that this looks and sounds and feels like PMS. I cross my fingers and smile just a little. Please god, let this be PMS.

They read:

Do you want me to give up?
Do you think you can get rid of me so easily?
I need you.
I miss you.
I think I love you.

I sigh. I stare at the monitor. I tell myself not to. I look down at the fading bruises on my knees. I close my eyes. I see a big nose. I see a rock-star chest. I hear a British accent that's getting easier to grasp with every passing day.

But then the lot of it is erased by five typed words: *I think I love you.*

I open my eyes. I open my mouth in protest. I open up the message.

"How do you feel about me?" Ian demands over our fifth Canadian Club and Canada Dry at Stex Haz.

We are having this decidedly Canadian happy hour because earlier, when Ian asked me why I was acting so strangely, I told him that I was terribly homesick and when he asked me for what, I couldn't actually think of anything specific, so I said: "Rye?"

"This menu is so Canadian," I say, smiling as though Ian has not just asked me this question, and as though I am not potentially pregnant, and as though Jack has not just written to say that He may love me. "It's like a bit of this and a bit of that"—I scan the nearby tables—"and none of it particularly well-done."

"Anna, how do you feel about me?" Ian asks again, this time in an embarrassed whisper. The rye seems to have ignited Ian's sentimentality. Or perhaps he senses competition—though I have told him nothing of Jack.

I take a deep sip of my drink and close the menu. "I like you," I say, quite adorably I think considering the circumstances.

He turns his head away from me, dismayed.

"What's wrong?"

He says: "I want to know how you feel about me."

I stare deep into his green-rimmed brown eyes. What is the name of that colour anyway? I slide my hand across the table and into his.

"What is it you want to hear?" I say softly, because I am still thinking about Jack's message, not to mention my absentee menstrual cycle which I now think may be karmic payback for the one I invented during the Londoner's visit.

"I don't want to *hear* anything. I want to know how you feel."

Hazel, I think again, though I know that this is not correct. This man has the most inexplicable eyes. I change direction. "How do *you* feel about *me*?" I ask, with what seems to me to be just the right amount of vulnerability.

His face tightens. "I like you."

It's that tone he always uses when he says these words to me—somewhere between pained and pleading. I wait for the qualifier and am rewarded.

"A lot."

"I like you too," I say.

The words hang too-brightly in the air. He sighs through his nose, looks away.

"Philip Morris *Super* Light?"

"No."

I light one for him anyway.

"It's kinda early for declarations, isn't it?" I say this because I don't have the answer he's looking for. Because there are too many answers. Because Jack just wrote and said He thinks He loves me and because I am late for my period and because honestly, I don't know what to think.

There is a Mickey D's across the street, obscenely fluorescent and bustling. I exhale loudly and turn to it. I feel Ian beside me. He is watching me closely now.

Where is my period? Where the fuck is my period?

I pass Ian the cigarette, extending my arm without turning my head. I hold it in the air, but I have to wait a long time before he reaches out to take it. When he does, I turn to him and our eyes lock.

The smoke billows up half-heartedly from the cigarette.

I quickly look away. I don't want him to see all the answers behind my eyes.

When we get back to Ian's flat, we run into his neighbour just outside the lift.

"*Csokolom*," the man says to me.

I nod my head. I wait until we're inside, then I whisper: "What the hell does that mean?"

"What does wha-at mean?" Ian asks, quite drunkenly really.

"Chock-a-lomb," I say. Incorrectly. "Sounds like some kinda curse or something."

Ian stares at me, then turns away. But not before I see the look of dismay spread across his face. He says: "It's a formal, respectful term. A greeting. It means I kiss your hand."

"Oh," I say. "Oh shit, that is so nice."

Ian softens. "Anna…"

And I can hear the rye in his voice: rye can make you say all sorts of things, things you don't mean, things you mean too much.

"I'm so tired," I say preemptively. "Rye makes me so very tired."

Ian closes his mouth. He breathes loudly through his nose, just once.

"You're just using me," he says later that night under the covers.

"Yes," I murmur. "For your telly and your stereo and your knowledge of local restaurants and your mind and, oh, let's not forget your body. Mmmm, this body."

He turns away. There is a strange silence.

"*You're* just using *me*," I whisper.

He turns back to me. He stares straight down his big nose at me. There is no trace of amusement on his face as he says: "For wha-at?"

Budapest Bytes is hoppin', so I am forced to sit at station twelve in the centre of the room where everyone can see my screen. I open up Yahoo.ca. I type in Pregnancy and Abortion and Holistic. I get seventy-two matches.

I scroll and scroll and scroll.

Teas and tinctures. Vitamins and herbs.

There are ways. I find ways. There are unreliable and unproven and crackpot ways. Not surprisingly, not a single one is endorsed by any sort of reputable medical authority. Clearly only the desperate and half-witted need apply here. Luckily, I am completely qualified.

But even the crackpots depend on a time frame. How many days? Weeks? I stare at my mini-calendar. I count days. I count weeks. I count condoms. I have no idea.

There are two more days until I'm thirty, twenty-three days till I have to leave Budapest. These I know, this I know. But potential length of potential pregnancy? No fucking clue whatsoever. Because we've been so careful. I swear to god we were totally careful.

I scroll and scroll and scroll.

Finally I settle on obscene amounts of ascorbic acid and/or parsley, because they seem semi-harmless and minimally insane, thought still not—it goes without saying—still not endorsed by qualified medical personnel. I carefully write out the formula and log off.

But I soon discover that pure Vitamin C isn't available in the drugstore here. And I can't even find a jar of dried parsley, never mind a clump of fresh.

I wander and wander and wander. I miss Canada like crazy. I miss convenience. I miss familiarity, similarity. I miss knowing where to buy fresh herbs even though I hardly ever exercised this right.

Finally, I purchase ten large Tetra packs of Orange Drink. I lug them to Ian's. I stare at them. I know they're of no use whatsoever. I clean out a mug and open container number one.

"There seems to be an excessive amount of crap juice in the refrigerator," Ian says when he gets home.

I shrug. "Got a craving." I guzzle the contents of my mug and refill from Tetra pack number three at my side.

My name is Anna Woods.

I am almost thirty and I am lying in bed at four in the morning with raging heartburn from the five packs of Orange Drink I have consumed in a pathetic bid to prevent what is still only a potential pregnancy. I listen to my lean and pasty and big-nosed British lover breathe beside me in the single bed that we share almost every night. I feel sick. I am sickened by this chain of events. I touch my belly, will the lifeblood out of my body. I miss Canada. I miss home.

How does one deal with such a situation in Budapest bloody Hungary?

My new British lover Ian breathes almost silently beside me. I have to strain to hear him. Even in his sleep this man is a mystery. How could I possibly have a child with this impenetrable man?

I miss Jack. Which is completely ludicrous considering the fact that I haven't even seen the guy in six years and He wasn't exactly Prince Charming even then.

Wriggling onto my side, I turn my face to the wall. I don't even like this person beside me, I realise. I do not, in fact, like Ian a lot. I'm not sure I like him at all. Though it must be admitted that I'm practically living with this person in the centre of Budapest, a city that was once two cities. And that I may be carrying his baby—*I may be the mother of his child.*

Perhaps I was a tad hasty in assuming I might be less of an idiot than I once was.

Spit is collecting at the back of my throat. I feel like I might throw up. I sit up quickly, then dash to the bathroom.

"You're green," a psychic once told me. "Growth, growth, growth. Green, green, green."

This is what I am thinking as I sit patiently by the toilet waiting to vomit the remainder of my five Tetra packs of Orange Drink. I can feel Ian in the next room feigning sleep.

Growth, growth, growth.

A fresh wave of nausea takes over.

Green, green, green.

But I had no idea that this was what she meant. I sure as hell never thought she could mean this.

"What are your intentions?" I blurt out when I return to the bedroom, no longer feeling green. (Nor orange.)

Ian lifts his head slowly from the pillow.

I sigh. I look away. "I think I'm pregnant."

"Wha-at?" he says in that British voice which makes the word sound as though it's two syllables, when really it's only one.

"Pregnant," I say.

"You're joking."

We stare at each other. I light a Philip Morris *Super* Light. I take a long drag. My stomach heaves. The taste in my mouth worsens.

"That's brilliant," he finally says, grinning. "That's bloody brilliant news!"

I glare at him, mid-exhale, then, smoke billowing out of my mouth, I say: "Wha-at?"

Ian is elated. "This is brilliant," he keeps saying. "Brilliant!"

It is six in the morning. I stare at him. I smoke.

"Spread the seed and all that," he says, actually beaming. "To be perfectly honest, I was a bit worried I might be a Jaffa."

"What's a jaffer?" I ask wearily, really quite tired of all this endless difference.

"An orange," he says impatiently. "A seedless orange. Don't you have those in Canada?"

I shrug. "If we do, we don't call them that."

He beams at me.

"Oranges," I say. "We just call them fucking oranges."

How likely is it that my travel insurance covers abortions, I wonder, staring again into the strangely horizontal shallows of Ian's Hungarian toilet bowl. Would this be considered an emergency? It does feel rather urgent.

It is 7 a.m. on the day before I turn thirty.

I must quit smoking until this is over, I think, realising that my early morning smoking extravaganza has triggered this bout of vomiting.

Not likely covered. No, I will undoubtedly have to shell out some serious *forints* for this one. Or perhaps even go home. Will I be forced to return home, I wonder with a thrill. Maybe I am just hungover, though I have never vomited the morning after in all of my sorry, liquor-saturated life. And unfortunately I didn't touch so much as a drop last night.

"Oh. Hi. Yeah, just got back really. Forced back to Canada for an abortion, which is not covered by goddamn travel insurance if you can believe. Anyway, I really didn't want to come back, but what's a girl to do?...Europe? Fantastic. I had the *best* time, well, as you can see, ha ha..."

This cannot happen. I cannot have this conversation. I cannot be pregnant. How can this *not* be an emergency?

We lie on the brown loveseat together, sipping lemony rye-and-gingers and watching videos while I purposefully smoke. It is the night before I turn thirty. In just a few hours, I will leave my twenties behind and become a freer, stronger, more sure kind of woman.

Ian says: "Perhaps you shouldn't smoke."

I light another.

Ian says: "Perhaps you shouldn't drink."

I take a deep gulp.

Ian says: "Perhaps you don't want to be pregnant."

"Give the man a prize."

Ian says: "Oh."

I smoke. I drink. I rest my head on his lap.

He says: "I didn't know."

I shrug.

He strokes my hair. His hands are gentle. It feels good. It feels peaceful. It feels light. There is an ease to lying here, watching videos—a familiar feeling, as though I'm not a traveller at all, as though I might still be at home.

"What are you planning to do?" he asks.

I shrug and try to decipher his tone—devilish or not devilish? I briefly envision lurid headlines, ridiculous court battles. How much should I tell this man? How much can I trust this indecipherable man?

He strokes my hair. "What are we going to do?" he asks.

I close my eyes. The problem is he's just so damn nice, that's all. He's just so *goddamn nice.*

Everything is a fucking mess.

My thirtieth birthday begins with a pregnancy test.

I lie still on the narrow bed, carefully holding in my morning pee while Ian stands in a pharmacy exchanging hand gestures with a Hungarian chemist. The Hungarian chemist does not speak much English, but quite commendably I think, is still attempting to give the necessary 'directions for use' for the home pregnancy test. So the two of them are struggling towards communication by way of such elementary words as *minute* and *urine* and the numbers *one* through *ten*. Just the thought of this pantomime makes me giggle. But then that makes me want to pee, so I stop. (I have no idea if morning pee is required for this test, but it *may* be, and frankly I cannot bear to wait another day in case it is. So here I am. Waiting. In agony. Trying not to laugh.)

Solemn things. I must think of solemn things. Like how there can be no question that Ian is what's commonly known as a nice fucking guy. Though one has to wonder if he is perhaps *too* nice. How badly does he want a baby? You hear of these deranged young men denying abortions to their girlfriends, or at least I'm sure I heard of one such case. Is Ian that sort of fellow? Are there warning signs I'm missing because of cultural miscommunication? But this is perhaps too solemn. I turn my focus to how seriously deplorable my hair has become. And how homesick I am, though I can't think of a single thing I'm missing specifically.

When Ian returns to the flat, he repeats the chemist's instructions. We take turns staring at the flimsy white wand, trying to laugh, trying to downplay its power.

"Okay," I finally say, grabbing hold of it roughly and making my way to the bathroom. "Put some music on or something so you don't hear me."

"Right," he says and turns toward the stereo.

I hurry to the toilet. The need to pee is beyond urgent. I straddle the bowl, gingerly position the plastic wand, and let go. A moment later the music starts.

The colour of my deplorable roots, I think.

When I am done, I carefully set the device on the edge of the tub. I flush. My watch reads: 10:06. I wash my hands

----

and walk into the living room on shaking knees. I drank too many rye-and-gingers last night; my head is hollow, dumb.

"Okay," I say.

Ian says: "Okay."

I light a cigarette. "Three minutes, right?"

"Right."

Ian is still beaming. I lean over quickly and kiss him. I wonder: How far would this man go?

"It'll be all right," he says.

"Yeah." But his fine and my fine are not exactly one and the same. I notice he has selected Tricky for our big moment. We listen to the music. "I'm sure it'll be fine."

"Perfectly fine." Ian sucks gleefully on his cigarette. "Is it time yet?"

My watch reads: 10:08. "One more minute," I say, feeling a sudden reluctance for this limbo period to end, a reluctance to reach the moment where only one of us will get what they want and *please please please let it be me.*

The clouds outside of Ian's giant apartment window seem to be clearing. In exactly one minute, I will find out if I'm pregnant.

Dans la maison du bonheur, la salle d'attente est la plus grande.

It comes to mind unbidden. From the Frenchman who once told me my hair was *parfait*, though things have obviously taken a sharp downward turn since then. But this waiting room, the one in which I am potentially impregnated by some Brit named Ian Wright and Jack Hammer is nowhere to be found, this waiting room is hardly in a house of good times. And why the hell am I taking counsel from the French anyway?

When I turn to Ian, he is beaming at me. Ian is so goddamn pleased. And then I wonder, just for a second, just for the merest of seconds, I wonder if maybe it wouldn't be

----

so bad. I wonder if maybe it would even be a good life: Ian and I and our foetus.

I am thirty.

It is my birthday.

I don't know what to think.

"Okay," I say, stubbing out my cigarette. I get up from the brown loveseat, aptly coloured and named, I now think.

Ian stands up as well.

"Stay here," I say, but he keeps following me. "Let me look on my own."

But still he is right behind me at the bathroom door.

I open the door. I bend over the tub. I stare at the plastic divining rod. "Two lines," I say. "Is that two lines?"

"'Tis."

"Two lines. That's good, right?"

"Depends on how you look at it really."

"Ian, *please*."

He looks down at the floor, sighs heavily. "Not pregnant," he says. "It means you're not pregnant."

I am grinning cautiously. "Not pregnant," I repeat.

Ian stares at the floor. I stare at the white wand. There is a drop of yellow urine near the handle. I feel a prissy stab of embarrassment.

"Thank Christ," I gasp, despite myself.

But Ian says nothing. He gives me a wan smile.

"Thank Christ," I say again with a whoosh of exhaled air.

We are moving now, the wand already so flimsy and foolish and so far behind us, moving back into the living room, sinking down onto the ugly, but appropriately coloured (I think) loveseat. I laugh nervously and with relief. I sneak glances at Ian. I look at him. I look away. Then I look at him again.

You almost had me, I think. *You almost fucking had me.*

"Oh my god," I say. "This is so fucking great!"

Ian looks forlorn.

I smile kindly. I smile with victorious empathy.

"It's too soon," I say.

He shrugs.

"This is the best birthday present ever!"

Ian smiles his wan smile. He hugs me, then leans back against the sofa and stares up at the ceiling. I don't know what he is thinking, but now I'm the one who can't stop beaming.

We reconvene at 6 p.m., because I claimed I had things to do, though actually I just wanted to spend the day grinning wildly and not feeling guilty about it. There are still clouds in the sky, but no rain, a general sombreness as opposed to the pointed one that will come later. But the weather doesn't bother me.

I arrive back at Ian's flat short of breath and full of hope in a way I have not felt in years. I am freshly blow-dried and outfitted in my best black duds. Ian hands me presents. We kiss and kiss and kiss, tasting of the homemade lemony rye-and-gingers Ian has prepared.

Ian leads me to a restaurant, one of the few we have not yet frequented together. He looks less forlorn than he was. Our meal is excellent despite the abysmal service. For dessert we share a piece of chocolate cake the likes of which neither of us has ever encountered. There is only one fork. Ian picks it up and feeds me with a focus that reminds me of something, though I can't think what exactly. Still, it is deeply familiar. I lean forward, moaning like a minx. We make predictable jokes about purchasing a vat of the rich chocolate sauce for later use at his flat.

"I like you a lot," Ian says softly and without pause and without looking up from the cake. "I am quite hooked."

"It must be my birthday," I smile coyly, because I'm never sure when he's being serious.

We lock eyes. You almost had me, I think, feeling suddenly strong and free and not pregnant. *You almost had me.*

I look away.

"Be careful," I whisper, though I wonder which of us I'm talking to.

He raises his eyebrows.

"I'm erratic," I say.

"I love erratic women. Turns me on."

We both pause, pretend not to notice the word love. His disappointment is palpable. This man is actually disappointed that I am not pregnant. What would he have done if I had been?

"You're so goddamn nice," I say, wearily now.

The cake finished, Ian scrapes the fork against the plate, deep in thought.

"How many times have you been in love?" he abruptly asks.

I wave my *Super* Light in the air. "Two. Maybe three. Depends what day you ask me."

"Maybe three? How can you have a maybe? Love's a smack in the head, not a maybe."

I say nothing. I totally agree. But the problem is, with someone like Jack (just for instance), you may not always want to admit to them once they're over. "What about you?"

"Three. Definitely three."

"Did you tell them?"

"That I loved them?"

I nod.

"Of course," he says. "Of course. Why? Did you love someone and not tell them? Is that the maybe three?"

I flush. I blush. I hesitate.

(Jack wrote: *I think I've always loved you.* Jack wrote: *I think you may be the one.*)

Ian pushes the empty cake plate across the table. It is practically licked clean. "Who was it?"

I flush. I blush. I hesitate.

He lights a smoke. "Tell me."

"It's not important. Why are we talking about this?"

"Tell me."

I sigh. I look away, hold out as long as I can, then look back.

Ian waits. Ian smokes. Ian stares at me with absolutely no expression on his face whatsoever.

"Tell me," he says.

So I tell him a little about Jack, a little about our past, a little about Him finding me just one year ago and then me being stood up twice in the last two months. I tell Ian that the main reason I came here was not really a vacation at all. It was to meet Jack.

Ian nods his head. Ian stubs out his cigarette. Ian shows nothing.

"My good fortune," he finally says. Then: "Do you still love him?"

I flush. I blush. I hesitate. "Hoooooo," I exhale. "Tough question. *That* is a really tough question."

Ian's brow—his whole face actually—is suddenly expectant and frozen.

"Tough question," I keep saying. (*Stop saying that.*) "I think I'm more in love with the idea of Him, the romanticised version of Him in my head. I don't know. To be honest, I don't know. I don't know who He is any more. But I can't say I feel nothing. Fuck, that's a *really* tough question."

Ian nods. Ian looks down at the table. Ian gulps at his pint.

I notice that it feels as though Jack is at the table with us now. As though He was just passing by and has now pulled up a chair to lean against.

"Am I ever going to see you again once you leave Budapest?" Ian finally asks. Because in less than a month I must leave Budapest. My ninety days are up. Though I could return. I could leave, see some opera and then return.

And I am overwhelmed by the sudden—unprecedented?—power that I have, that this question, these questions have revealed. Feeling suddenly strong and free and not pregnant, I think: I can hurt this person, this person who *actually wanted me to have his child*! And maybe because Jack is here at the table with us now, because Jack brings out the mean in me, encourages it even, I have to restrain myself from lashing out. I savour just a little bit the overpowering urge to hurt, but then I look at Ian's face, which is so big-nosed and hopeful and familiar in that foreign but recognisable way, that all I can do is go halfway.

I say: "I don't know."

Ian instantly turns back to his lager, drinking half of it in a single gulp. He signals for the bill. The waiter ignores him.

Still I am talking. "That's the honest answer," I say. "That's honest. It doesn't mean I won't, but it doesn't mean I will either. I don't know, Ian. *I don't know.*"

Because this is the truth.

I reach across the table for his hand, but he withdraws it, picks up his glass and drains the last of his lager. I pick up his lighter instead, as though I was never reaching for his hand anyway, and start methodically flipping it on our white linen tablecloth.

Jack. Ian. Jack. Ian. Ja-

Despite the fact that he is now looking at me, I make a point of staring down at the blue lighter, probably the same lighter he used on the sidewalk the day we bumped into each other. This man actually wanted me to be pregnant. And isn't that the sort of man you'd want to have a child with? Well? Isn't it?

Say ass, I think. I love it when you say ass.

I am thirty.

It is my birthday.

"I don't want this to end," he says.

But all I can think is that there are too many people at this table. I shrug. I am confused. I am terribly confused. I cannot think straight with all of these people.

"You're just so goddamn nice," I whisper.

Flip, flip, flip goes the lighter.

(Jack wrote: *I think I've always loved you.* Jack wrote: *I think you may be the one.*)

And when I finally do look up, Ian is no longer looking at me, but at the bill. His expression is horribly grim.

Ian is holding my hand, but furious. I can see he is upset. Any fool can see.

"You're upset," I say, but he says nothing, leading me, as always, through these Budapest alleyways, but now and for the first time leading me angrily. "Talk to me."

"Do you even like me?" he says, stopping now to push me up against a wall.

"I like you," I say too quickly. (She doth protest too much.) "Why would you ask that?"

He looks away, his face scrunched up in an ugly sneer.

"I like you," I say. (Again!)

And now he looks back, his face so fierce and sceptical.

"I don't want you to think..."

But I cannot finish. What would I say? That I am using him? That I have been using him? That I was alone in Budapest and I just wanted to be with someone, anyone? Or that I needed a love story to take home with me like a fucking souvenir? Or that I just wanted to be in love, but not pregnant and is that so wrong? Or that part of me wishes there had only been one line on this morning's test, that maybe there *should* have been only one line?

I pull him into my arms. "I like you," I say. "It's just-"

And I search now for some kind of plausible explanation, for something to dispel his anger even if only for this one night.

"I don't do this," I hear myself saying. "I don't open up to people. I've been single for four years. I don't know *how* to be with another person. Or if I even want to."

And I can feel, even as I begin to hate myself, that it is working. That Ian's body is relaxing against me. That this is a sufficient and plausible explanation, and maybe even, at least partially, the truth.

How I loathe these sufficient and plausible explanations.

"I'm terrible at this," I say, launching into cliché. "It's not about you or how much I like you. It's about me."

I hate myself. I kiss his neck. And at that moment, I wonder: Why is it that I *know* I like you more than I *feel* I like you? I strain towards him.

He takes a step back from me. "I think I understand," he finally says in the softest possible voice.

A ripple of fear passes through me. And as we resume our walk through the dark and uneven streets, a light rain (but not the shattering one that will come later) just now beginning to fall, an uneasy tension walks with us.

Jack at least is falling behind. I can feel Him backing the hell off.

Just how much *does* Ian understand, I wonder. And if he really does comprehend the situation, could he explain it to me?

We wrap our arms around each other and let our hips jostle as we walk. We pretend that everything is all right, that neither of us is re-evaluating. It's easier that way. It's less hassle. Passersby must simply see two people in love.

Just two happy people. One happy couple. They must not even notice that there is a third person lurking behind us, a large American slouching languidly in the filthy shadows.

"I think I understand," Ian says again.

The night of my thirtieth birthday there is an apocalyptic rain. And I cannot help but wonder what would have happened if there had not been such a rain, if it had been a typically broiling late July evening instead. Would it all have come out different? Would everything still have shifted or would it have stayed the same—getting harder and drier like the dog shit baking on the pavement?

But I'll never know. There was an unforgiving rain on the night of my thirtieth birthday. It roared through my ears and made me feel alive because someone reminded me that I was. It was cold and it was wet and it was gorgeous. And just the sheer presence of it, the unbridled force of it seemed to change everything between Ian and I.

He said: "Isn't this a gorgeous rain."

And it was. It really was.

Ian is silent until we get to Old Man's Pub where we first met, making out on the dance floor as I tried to avoid the Londoner. (Also where I met the Frenchman.) Ian orders us each a shot of Unicum and a pint of Dreher.

We sit down at one of the tables in the corner. The music is barely tolerable. We watch the crowd a little—desperate, drunk, horny. There is a feverish determination and purpose to this crowd. That used to be us, I think. That used to be me. But I am full of denials even before I am done thinking this thought.

Ian is yelling at me from across the table.

"You've probably slept with way more people than I have."

I stare at him. "Wha-at?"

He downs his shot. "Right then," he says, getting up and sliding sideways between his chair and the wall to get free.

I turn around, watch him fight his way up to the bar. I stare back at the wall across from me where he was recently seated. What the hell was that?

A new song starts up. I cock my head and try to place it. I smile. The *Grease* soundtrack. *You're The One That I Want.*

Ian slides his twenty-nine-inch waist back into his chair, pushes a second shot of Unicum towards me and downs his own. He turns to me with a devilish grin. "Go on. What's your strike zone?"

I sip my Dreher, still pleased by this song that I haven't heard in just forever. The crowd is going crazy for it.

"Are you going to drink those?" Ian asks, pointing at my two untouched shots of Unicum. I shake my head. Ian picks them up and downs them in quick succession. He takes a long haul off his Dreher. "Right then. All you do is figure out the highest and lowest age differences of the people you've slept with, at the time you slept with them, and add them together."

I sigh.

"Of all the people you've slept with."

"What's going on here?" I ask.

"Mine's seven," he says.

"Seven."

"Go on."

I shake my head. I light a cigarette. I stare at the crowd.

"How old's Jack then?" Ian asks, his face still a blank slate.

I suck on my cigarette. I sip my beer. I think: I'll take a half-kilo of less, please. Please, isn't there some way to remove some of this flesh?

Sorry, ma'am, but that operation is not covered by your insurance.

I sigh. "What's going on here?"

Ian shrugs and smiles. Ian shows nothing. Ian says: "Just making conversation."

He is terribly drunk.

"Gorgeous," he slurs, turning his big-nosed face up to the pummelling rain that greets us as we exit the meat market below. "Isn't this a *gorgeous* rain?"

He loves this word gorgeous, uses it for everything I now realise. Not just me. He weaves down the centre of the street, his arms spread wide open.

My instinct is to hunch my shoulders, to walk as quickly as possible to the nearest available shelter. And though I was just about to make a disparaging remark about the pissy weather coinciding with my thirtieth goddamn birthday, I too turn my face up and am instantly soaked. I feel a rush of delight. I surrender. The rain is bouncing forcefully off of everything: the street, the cars, our skin. This rain is not fooling around.

It *is* gorgeous, I think. It *is* a goddamn gorgeous rain.

"This is gorgeous," Ian is still saying as he stumbles down the road.

I hurry up to him and pull one of his hands down into mine, but he is careful to keep looking up into the sky for another beat before he turns his face to me. I smile seductively. He doesn't seem to notice. We stroll together in the downpour, holding hands in the middle of a cobblestone street now shining a wet black—even in the broken spots.

He has made it gorgeous because he said so, I realise. This is a goddamn good man to be around. I squeeze his limp hand. The city lights bounce yellow off the shining ground.

I am grinning.

I am pleased.

I am thirty.

And then suddenly Ian is pushing me up against the side of a building. Roughly. He pushes me roughly, and already his hand is down inside my skirt and underpants, and he is touching me, touching me, touching me, staring indecently into my eyes as I stare at him, shocked. The bouncers outside of the club could see us if they turned. Ian blocks their view with his thin, twenty-nine-inch-waisted body. He pushes that body hard against me and his fingers are inside me and his hand is—

A car passes.

"Stop," I gasp.

But he doesn't.

My knees begin to shake. I clutch onto his shoulders with my arm, trying to catch my breath in the crushing rain and the lights shining so bright off of the street, until I hear footsteps and suddenly his hand retreats and I am sucking in air and Ian is holding me benignly as the stranger passes.

"Jesus Christ," I say, but already he is pulling me back out onto the street by my hand.

My legs won't move. My legs are shaky. My legs are not all right.

Jesus Christ.

Still the rain shatters the quiet of the night.

When we turn the corner and come upon a dark entranceway, Ian pulls me in. But instead of touching me, he calmly, maybe even coolly lights a Philip Morris *Super* Light.

"You Brits," I say, quite unable, it would seem, to stop generalising. "Proper by day, properly deviant by night."

He ignores me.

"How can you smoke at a time like this?" I ask, reaching out for him with some desperation. He holds me off, casually smoking, smoking casually as I try and try and try to reach his lips with my own, to match up any part of my body with his.

It goes on.

Finally he turns to me and speaks with a malicious sneer that cuts through the black gloom and the sound of the rough rain and even my pathetic scrabbling. "Tell me you want me," he hisses.

I say nothing. I stare at this new person, this not-so-nice person as he slips his hand just inside my waistband and stops it.

"Tell me you want me," he hisses again, something fiendish in his eyes, something foreign.

"I want you," I whisper, pushing his hand down. "I want you."

He smiles—maybe even meanly though it's difficult to tell in the dark. He pulls me into the middle of the deserted street. He pushes my skirt up. Before I know what's happening, he has sunk to his knees and is pulling my knickers down to my ankles. There is a shattering rain beating down on me, falling so densely I imagine little bruises popping up all over my skin. I look around to see if anyone else is out, if anyone might be watching, but rain splashes distort my glasses and I cannot see a thing.

I give in and turn my face up to the sky, letting the rain pound down on my forehead, my cheeks, my nose, my chin. My hair is soaked. I lightly touch his shoulder with my hand. He is on his knees. I cannot see anything.

The rain falls.

I feel and I feel and I feel.

Laughing.

"We were in the middle of a lit street for god's sake!"

And he laughs too now. For some reason, he is laughing now too. "Dob utca to be precise."

"Mr. Wright!" I say, my arm linked in his as we shuffle home. "What has gotten into you?"

He stops. He hooks his hands behind my back and leans back to look at me. He is smiling, tired, drenched. So am I. We grin at each other with our hands clasped behind the other's back. And then quite unrealistically, quite ridiculously, quite *impossibly*, he spins. He is spinning. And so am I. Spinning with him, spinning in his arms.

Rain surrounds us, falls between us, flies off of us.

Are we in a movie, I wonder. This is a cheesy movie scene. But I cannot think which one and Ian is not the person to ask.

I laugh and laugh and laugh.

Dizzy.

And I think: These are things Jack and I would do. Jack and I would do these things, but we wouldn't spin. No, there definitely wouldn't be any spinning involved. But then why am I thinking about Jack?

When we are almost home, Ian pulls my hand and makes me run, splashing his feet down hard in all of the puddles so that the water sprays up and out at me. We are laughing and squealing and I feel so much like a kid that I don't even recognise the feelings I'm feeling.

Is this real? Can he even be real?

Spinning spinning spinning…

I feel like I've just been hit in the head.

In the lift, dizzy and drenched, we kiss until long after we reach his floor. Inside his flat, we strip down. We are too tired to speak. Too much has already been said.

It is the end of my birthday.

I am thirty.

This is me at thirty.

Ian takes his time selecting the music, finally settles on a mixed tape. I wait silently on the loveseat until he presses Play. He sits down beside me and leans back while I lean forward. His hand rests on my lower back. Both of us smoke. We listen to a James song about rain. We stare out of Ian's gigantic open window and listen to the real rain outside that is as loud as the rain song on the stereo.

My hair drips onto my bare skin. I start to shiver. There is a foreign buzzing in my stomach, something warm and satisfying, but unfamiliar.

Spinning, spinning, spinning...

This is better than Jack, I think. This is better than anything I have ever known.

Feeling so much like a kid I don't even recognise what I'm feeling...

Suddenly I notice the grin on my face. I'm happy. I realise suddenly that I am happy. Happy right now, I think, shivering. Not thinking I should be happy or thinking I will be happy or thinking I'm gonna be happy in just another minute or so if I just try a little harder.

I am just plain happy.

So suddenly.

So strongly.

So intensely.

And I cannot remember the last time I felt like this. I don't think I have ever felt like this. My stomach hums soothingly. I turn to Ian, amazed. "I'm so happy right now," I say. Softly. Amazedly. Truthfully.

He slowly turns his head from the rain that so recently engulfed us and the gigantic window that frames it. And shivering, I reach out to him, skin happily outstretched. But at the same moment that the James/rain song ends, I sense Ian flinching. Flinching away from me. He gets up and walks over to the stereo. His profile is a grimace. His eyes are distant. He says nothing.

I stare at him, my mouth slack.

Flinching away from me.

My recent happiness is gone. My recent happiness lasted approximately 2.3 seconds. When a man flinches from your touch, things are probably not all right.

Ian hits Rewind. He keeps his back to me until the electronic grinding comes to a halt. He presses Play and then, without turning, and in the silence before the James/rain song starts up again, he says: "I lied."

I am drenched and dazed and dripping on his loveseat. I mumble something like: "Huh?"

"About the test. I lied." Ian turns. "Two lines aren't really okay. Two lines means you're pregnant."

The rain song blares. He reaches over to turn it down slightly.

"It's...the thing is, I wanted you to have a nice birthday," Ian is saying. "I didn't want you to worry. And I figured you might be sad if it really was negative, so then you'd see..."

I stare out the window at a rain I cannot see for the darkness. Pregnant. Thirty. The 'TESL wanker's' fucking baby.

"A fucking 'TESL tot'," I whisper.

There is a long silence, then Ian says: "What?"

"A fucking 'TESL tot'," I say again and then burst into hysterical, shivering laughter.

Ian emerges from the shower the next morning looking terribly earnest and purposeful. He says: "I reckon we ought to talk about what we're going to do."

I put down my guidebook. "You totally read my mind. I was thinking Eger."

Ian frowns. "Eger?"

"Oh is that how you say it? Yeah, Eger. I was just reading about it in my guidebook and apparently it's a

----

typical Hungarian town, and it's not too far. Plus it's famous for its wine cellars and its wine—they call it Bull's Blood. Creepy, huh? Anyway, I was thinking this weekend or maybe next week."

"Honestly, Anna. What are we going to do?"

"Well if you don't want to go there we could always –"

"Anna! Don't you remember last night?"

Ian looks exhausted. Ian looks terribly tired. I think this vacation would do Ian a world of good. I pick up my guidebook. "Or we could always try this place. God I don't know how to say it either: P, E, C..."

He starts to laugh through his nose. He shakes his head. "Eger, yeah. Sounds bloody marvellous. Count me in for Eger."

I smile triumphantly.

"Now what about this pregnancy business?"

"What pregnancy business?"

"My bun in your oven, Anna. You're pregnant."

"Is this some kind of weird British humour thing?"

Ian sighs.

"You Brits are so weird. Wasn't it you that told me you were a Jaffa?"

Ian stares at me until I look away.

"No, I'm not pregnant, silly. How could I be? Now do you think we should take the bus or the train? The bus is cheaper, but the train..."

Ian's not really taking this blow to his manhood very well. He is adamant that I'm pregnant, even though those two lines were as clear as day—I saw them myself! I feel sorry for him in a way. After all, his intentions are so sweet.

Maybe that's why I feel so close to him lately. I miss him terribly these days. I miss him even when he is only at work, even when he's teaching a class that will probably last but a few hours. I feel that sickness in my belly, the one that I have worked so hard to avoid—single for four years. It's not just loneliness, it's sudden loneliness, sudden contrast: alone and not alone, happy and not happy. It hurts. How can it hurt to be away from someone for three hours?

I lie on our narrow bed.

I smell him in the bed sheets.

I stare at the impossibly large window, which is practically ours now, but I keep the shutter down. I no longer want or need or am able to see through the window. I no longer need to be seen.

I do nothing but ache for him.

I can smell him on me. Taste too. I put off showering, brushing my teeth, washing my face so that this smell, this taste will stay on me, around me, inside of me.

This is love. This is the smell of love: mixed-up layers of sweat, funky and salty and almost unpleasant. This is such an original thought, feeling, experience, I think, knowing that it is not and wondering why it still has to be so goddamn painful, why I still cannot discern any sort of expression on his face at all, why he still seems so different from everyone I know, and most of all, why he seems to be retreating from me ever so slightly with every passing day.

For some reason, I am now the one with the pleading voice when I say, "I like you. A lot." And he is the one with the distant look in his eye, perhaps seeing a place as far away and yet as near as Seattle, perhaps seeing one line where there were actually two, perhaps merely seeing my deplorable hair.

I am thirty.

My name is Anna Woods.

Rain pours constantly through my head.

And the dog howls. (It's like leave a message already.)

I feel less strong, less free, less independent than I ever did. I call him Mr. Wright. First and foremost because that is his name, but also because I am pleading with him now. My every word is a plea. A plea for him to snap out of it, because in sixteen days, I have to leave Budapest. In sixteen days, my time here is up. And shouldn't we be making the best of what time we have left together?

Though, as Ian pointed out, I could always leave, take in some opera, and then come right back. Course it must also be admitted that he hasn't pointed this out as of late. These days his only topic of conversation seems to be pregnancy—pregnancy, pregnancy, pregnancy. (And I thought I was obsessive.)

Poor fellow. Probably feels a sense of failure or something. I really do feel for him, especially since his failure ensures my success.

The driver on the bus that Ian and I take to Eger—where we will undoubtedly sample copious amounts of locally-produced wine, which I pray will aid in the revival of Ian's flagging interest in me—this driver has turned up the radio, presumably due to, or at the very least coinciding with, the opening strains of Bonnie Tyler's *Total Eclipse of the Heart*. And there is a woman in a long cotton dress in the seat ahead of me who is tapping her finger to this appalling and so not timeless Bonnie Tyler song.

This has got to be one of the worst songs ever recorded, I think. And I say that after *What a Feeling* played not ten minutes ago. I say that in what must surely be the full throes of love. Because despite the driver, despite the song, I am happy. So cautiously happy.

Ian's head is resting on my shoulder. He is napping on the bus while I am forced to listen to this disturbing tune. Ian seems so tired lately, so very exhausted, while I am the opposite: still dizzy, still spinning, still in love. But cautiously now, carefully now. Because Ian is very tired lately. Ian seems so permanently exhausted, and I don't want to disturb the poor fellow. He already seems so very disturbed.

Frankly we find it difficult to even get to the wine cellars.

Our room in Eger not only has a double bed, but—luxury of luxuries—a television with MTV and Sky News and an Extreme Sports channel which, I soon discover, is running a feature on British Columbia's skate parks. I am surprisingly soothed by the sight and sound of my fellow Canadians, even if they are West Coasters and I have nothing in common with them. And then I realise that this is the first time in my life that I have ever felt like a fellow Canadian. But I am so cautiously in love with Ian that I refuse to even feel homesick any more.

I flip channels.

Flip. Flip. Flip.

Beside me, Ian naps. He is so tired lately, but I don't mind. It feels nice. Cozy. What a nice, cozy couple we make, I think, feeling suddenly light and clean and not even caring how dependent on his presence I've become.

Flip. Flip. Flip.

Half of the cellars are closing by the time Ian and I find them, but as we have not yet eaten dinner, we soon catch up to the dregs of the more timely tourists. Ian's delusions of fatherhood are growing increasingly tiresome.

"Are you sure you ought to be drinking?" he asks me for the tenth time.

I roll my eyes and fetch us another round. He accepts it without expression when I return. I reach for his hand. It rests warmly in mine, though he does not reciprocate my squeeze.

"I'm so happy we came," I say with (I think) a winning smile.

He nods but says nothing. His bleary eyes scan the people around us as I fetch cup after cup of dense Bikaver wine.

When the room starts to sway, we rise as best we can and begin the long walk back to the hotel. There is a slight delay when I bend over at the top of a winding hill and vomit neatly into a ditch (an event which I suspect will not help in the interest revival), but otherwise the journey is uneventful until we reach the hotel.

"Look at the flags," I say quite drunkenly and indignantly really.

Ian shuffles beside me, a lifeless arm around my waist.

"Look at those fucking flags."

He looks up then at the flags hanging listlessly off the front of our hotel. "Christ, I'm knackered," he finally slurs.

"France, Germany, England, America, Japan. What is that, Spain?"

Ian belches wetly.

"Where the fuck is Canada?" I shout, quite angry really, not to mention frustrated by Ian's waning interest. "It really pisses me off that you never see the Canadian flag anywhere."

Ian looks from me to the flags and back again. He weaves a little against me. He is even pastier than usual. "Maybe it's too new," he says, his eyes possibly even clearing a little. (Or perhaps crossing.)

"What do you mean *too new?*"

"Well you only adopted the maple leaf in the sixties."

"We did?"

"Mid-sixties I believe."

(Definitely crossing.)

"It was the Red Ensign before," he says.

"How do you know this? Is it some kind of British thing?"

He shrugs. "Bloody O Level."

"But why don't I know this?"

Ian shrugs again.

I turn back to the flags. There is a gentle breeze now. They flutter reluctantly.

He says: "More likely it's implied."

"Im-plied?"

His eyes dart once. "America," he says. "It's implied by the American flag, or even the Union Jack. English-speaking and all that."

I stare at him. I am suddenly and completely repulsed by this man. This man who is fooling himself so completely, this man who has no idea who I am, this man who will never understand me and how could I ever have thought otherwise? "Im-plied," I repeat.

"At least you have a flag. Mine's a bloody racist emb-"

"You don't understand," I mutter. "You'll never understand."

We do not touch each other that night. I flip channels instead.

Flip. Flip. Flip.

Apparently, while sleeping in a double bed, no touching is actually necessary. Which is just as well considering that Ian passed out immediately upon our arrival and I am still fairly pissed off about the flag business.

Flip. Flip. Flip.

But then back at his place, in his (practically our) narrow single bed, is it only a lack of spatial options that leads to stroking, cuddling, goddamn spooning? Is that the only reason for skin on skin? Doesn't he care about me at all?

Flip. Flip. Flip.

The only downside about shifting into love, I realise, lying here going from channel to channel, is that you can shift right back out of it as well.

Shift. Shift. Shift.

One second I'm in love.

The next I'm repulsed.

And then I'm in love again—with one or the other.

No wonder I was so goddamn dizzy.

Flip. Flip. Flip.

Frankly I can't wait to get back to Budapest.

He is wooing me again, my Jack. Wooing me with old memories this time. *Remember when,* He now writes, suddenly eager to invoke our past, perhaps sensing in some atavistic male way, even from as far away as Seattle that there is a battle to be fought now. That He needs to make a stand, plant a flag. That there may be another.

Though I have told Him nothing of Ian.

Remember how we got carried away on someone's front lawn that night, and morning traffic started going by, and then a police cruiser pulled up and we ran away, and as we ran away we saw those little Pesticide signs sticking up out of the grass.

And I do remember.

Remember that night on that patio when you demanded I give you my number. You were wearing something soft, velvet maybe. You reminded me of some evil cartoon character. The passion. The fervor. The silliness. That was an awesome night.

And I don't actually remember this, but it seems likely enough.

Remember that night at that booze-can when...

It goes on.

And I allow myself to be wooed, letting typed words trigger old and dark and well-worn emotions, being wooed by Jack even as I stare pleadingly at Ian, straining forward and then back across an eerie, tired quiet, not knowing how I feel nor how I will feel and maybe even unsure of how I ever felt.

Maybe the only reason I have told Jack nothing of Ian is because I would not know what to say. What would I possibly say?

We were so good together, Jack writes. *Do you remember?*

And I do. Unfortunately I do. Though I'm not sure good is the right word.

Shift. Shift. Shift.

The headline would read 'Anna Woods, 30,' I realise as Ian and I sit in an ancient chair lift sauntering up an enormous hill near Buda so that we can get a spectacular and all-encompassing view of the whole of the once-divided, once-two-separate-cities Budapest. (As if you can ever see *all* of anything.)

In just nine days I must leave Budapest. Though so far I have made no plans at all in this regard. And though Ian and I do not discuss it, everything we do feels weighted with finality. Is this the last time we'll do this together? And this? And this? And this?

This is beyond perilous, I think now, staring down between my feet into someone's well-tended garden below.

"When do you think these things were last safety-inspected?"

Ian shrugs, puts a limp and scrawny arm around me.

I continue to stare down at the ground. "If we fell from here, at least we would only be horribly crippled."

"Don't worry. It gets worse."

The trees brush against our feet and arms as the chair glides unsteadily over treetops that have been cleared only enough for us—or people like us—to pass. The chairs on our right, going down the hill, look surreal: brightly-hued couples gliding past dense greenery on rickety tent-pole metal.

"This is kinda *Crouching Tiger, Hidden Dragon*," I say. "When they're swaying and fighting in the bamboo."

"What's *Crouching Tiger…?*"

I am half-delighted and half-irritated with this answer. How can I (at times) love a person who is not cinema savvy? Although I too am quite out of the loop now, aren't I? I haven't seen a movie mag in months, no longer recognise the latest titles. It may just be the disaster that was Eger that is irritating me. After all it was Ian's idea to come here today and he hasn't proposed any joint ventures since before my thirtieth birthday.

"It's gorgeous," he said this morning. "It's romantic."

And I wondered if his indifference might not be fading at last.

"Look back," Ian says now, already twisted around on his side of the chair.

I clutch frantically at the metal bar as the chair sways. "No way. I do not look back." *(Ha!)*

"It's gorgeous," Ian sighs wearily.

"If we died, if this chair plummeted to the ground right now, the headline would read: 'Canadian Anna Woods, *thirty!*'"

"'…and her young British lover, Ian Wright.'"

I punch his arm. "Cheeky bugger."

He smiles.

The chair rocks dangerously.

Once we reach the top (following a clumsy dismount by yours truly), we walk up a short, but deceptively steep incline and arrive at an old stone lookout tower. There are two flights of stairs, which we wheezily climb.

The view here is supposed to be breathtaking, but it has turned hazy and we can't see anything at all. We lean over the railing, panting. As per usual, I'm hungover. As per usual, Ian is hungover and tired. He sits on a stone bench carved into the wall. I lie down beside him, my head resting on his lap. We say nothing to each other. Lately we are surrounded by an eerie quiet.

I stroke his unshaven cheek. "Rough," I say. "*Rrrrr-uffff.*"

"Gur," he says, but all it sounds like is a proper word: gur.

I laugh. "What is that?"

"I'm growling."

"That is not a growl. That is a gur."

He shrugs. "I can't make animal noises like you." He leans his head back against the cool stone, refuses to look at me.

I have offended this man for no reason whatsoever. It's no wonder he doesn't care for me at all. I close my eyes quickly, remember the sound the husky made after it got hit on the street outside of my hotel/apartment. The way it howled. How funny that we're trying to make animal noises while it made a decidedly human sound. And then I realise that I still don't know if it was the car or the truck that hit it. Was it the car or was it the truck? I feel an unease I cannot place. Just what in the hell was that husky trying to tell me anyway?

Ian strokes my hair, my deplorable hair. Ian is so goddamn nice. Ian is just so *fucking nice.*

"Are you thinking about Jack?" he asks quietly and without— or so it sounds—a predetermined opinion.

"No! Why would you ask that?"

He shrugs and continues to stare straight ahead. "You were smiling. You had a strange smile on your face."

I shake my head. "No."

He shrugs again, lights a cigarette and inhales deeply. He looks bone-tired. "You seem a bit off lately."

I sigh, decide not to mention how tired he's been.

"Anna," he says gently, looking down at me. "If He was here right now, in Budapest...whose bed would you be in?"

I look away. This is the first time he has mentioned Jack since my birthday. I reach into my purse for one of my own Philip Morris *Super* Lights and light it slowly, carefully. He is patiently watching me, thick bags under his indecipherable eyes. There is nowhere to hide here. You can see everything. I shiver.

"Yours," I say and watch as the bags under his eyes instantly disappear, and then unexpectedly: "I think."

His face hardens. "You think?"

"I'm pretty sure," I say, horrified, words bypassing brain matter.

"Pretty sure."

"Yours," I say again.

Ian blinks. "You think."

I study the thick air.

Ian sighs. "When do you have to leave?"

"By the twelfth I guess."

"What's today?"

"The third."

Ian makes a low, non-committal sound in his throat. The bags have deepened under his eyes.

"Do you want me to go now?" I whisper.

"I'm not chucking you out or anything."

The fog seems to be getting thicker. "But you want me to go."

"Did I say that?"

"No."

Ian sighs wearily. "I think we ought to get married."

"What?"

"Married."

I blink at him.

"Anna, you're pregnant. I'm not fooling around. This isn't some cultural misunderstanding. That test said you were pregnant, as in having a baby. Now pull yourself together. What are we going to do?"

He's telling *me* to pull myself together? I stare up at him. "I'm having a baby?"

"Yes."

"I'm pregnant?"

"Yes!"

"Oh my god, are you serious?"

"Yes!"

"Oh my god," I whisper.

"Exactly."

"Ian, what am I gonna do?"

"Let's get married. Marry me."

"Marry you? We hardly fucking know each other."

"Of course we do. We're having a baby."

"Jesus Christ, Ian. One thing at a time. *Jesus Christ.* This is a total fucking shock, I'll tell you that much. I thought you were fucking delusional or taking the piss or something. You know, I'm not sure I'm clear on taking the piss."

"But I told you I wasn't."

"Yes, but you Brits and your dry humour, who can be sure?"

"Anna, what are you gonna do?"

I stare straight up into his big-nosed and pasty British face. "Jesus Christ, Ian. I only found out about three seconds ago. Gimme a minute, all right?"

He looks away, staring into the mist over Budapest.

Jesus Christ!

And then I hear it again.

"Do you hear that?"

Ian turns to me. "Wha-at?"

"A dog. Can't you hear a dog?"

Ian shakes his head.

"I swear to god I can hear a dog howling...a dog...a dog...calling to me..." I stub out my cigarette and sit up. "You don't hear it?"

Ian narrows his eyes. "No, Anna. I don't hear any bloody dog."

Marry Ian.

Have Ian's baby.

Now that's crazy, I think, walking towards Budapest Bytes so that Ian can take a nap and I can take a moment to try and fucking *think*.

Although it must be admitted that he has his qualities. He does have a whole series of good qualities. How nice he is. How often he surprises me. How right from our first date he made me feel gorgeous and asked when he could see me again and loved my hair even after it was so hopelessly damaged and how he squirted vodka and Bomba into my mouth and how the sex just keeps getting better and better and how he could pull me up under a bridge, a beautiful bridge in Budapest goddamn Hungary at four in the morning and how we could shag under one of the supports with cars roaring by below and just ten feet away and how beautiful the Danube was and how much I liked him telling me that he liked me, a lot, and how great that birthday cake was and how he could turn an apocalyptic rain into something transcendant just by saying so and how even someone, or maybe especially someone who was not part of the plan and who I could not figure out though he was strangely familiar, how someone like this could make me feel so alive, so beautiful, so dizzy, so human, so not terrible...*so gorgeous.*

Because he tells me so.

And let us not forget his charming pronunciation of the word ass.

Speaking of which, what about Jack? What about Jack fucking Hammer? Are you thinking about Jack, Ian had asked, even though I was not. Not right then anyway. Not until he mentioned Him that is. But then Jack is never far from the surface, is He? Is He?

It's not that I've been dishonest. It's just that I feel two things—separately and together and at unpredictable and uncontrollable moments. I feel for two men. I feel for two men at once and how do you reconcile that? Just marry the first one to knock you up? Is that the answer? Are you just supposed to flip a coin and stay with someone because there will always be good days and bad days and it's only the number of days that matter and there is no real *one*?

No really, I'm asking.

I shuffle into Budapest Bytes. It's virtually empty. I take a corner terminal and log on. I have four messages in my inbox: three of them are junk mail, the fourth is from Jack Hammer. I open it, annoyed.

It reads: *Could only get a flight to Vienna. Arrive Aug 7ᵗʰ. Choose a rendezvous point. Jack.*

I stare over the monitor at the place where two walls intersect. It is Aug. 3rd.

Decide: The 'TESL wanker' or the asshole.

I stare blankly at the walls.

The American or the Brit.

No really, decide.

There is an old triangular stain burrowed into the drywall.

I think: Ian.

I think: Jack.

I think: Either Ian or Jack.

But honestly, all I want to do is run.

"I have to leave," I say to Ian over chocolate cake and coffee at Articzoka the next day. We have come back for our own final slices of that unearthly birthday cake, but it is not the same. The charge is gone as we feed ourselves our own damn cake, and besides, I'm eating for two now—how not sexy is that?

Ian doesn't seem terribly bothered by the inferior quality of the cake. He looks up mid-moan and I wonder if his satisfaction is feigned or sincere. And if sincere, did he ever truly feel the full intensity of the cake we shared on the night of my birthday?

Since the chair lift yesterday, things have been unbearably pleasant. We have been playing way too fucking nice. I look away.

He puts down his fork. I feel his hand on my knee under the table. "What do you mean?" he says.

"I have to go away early. To Vienna. I need to think."

He frowns.

I shrug, clear my throat. "Jack," I say. "Jack wants to meet me there and...and I have to go."

The hand withdraws from my knee. He puts down his fork. It clatters against the plate. He stares at it. I cannot tell if he is pleased or pissed off. "Your honesty is...impeccable," he finally says, then: "When?"

"Tomorrow. I think it's best if I go tomorrow."

"Yes," he replies. "Yes, quite right."

And I think how appropriate—though undeserved obviously—how appropriate it might be for him to ask me now when he can see me again. I wait quietly, patiently.

When can I see you again?

But he says nothing. He looks exhausted. Is he pleased or is he pissed off? The ice cream slowly melts on our separate plates. Somewhere outside a car alarm blares angrily, reminding me of that first night on his loveseat.

He doesn't even ask about the baby. But then what if there is no baby? Just how reliable is a Hungarian home pregnancy test anyway? (Again with the boorish North American tourist.)

Ian is not looking at me, so I sneak a peek at him. There is something in his face that reminds me of the dog, again that damn dog that barrelled past me all those weeks ago on that narrow sidewalk and how, only moments later, it was hit by a car or a truck or by some kind of moving vehicle at least.

I cock my head.

The dog howls.

I can hear it as clearly as I did that afternoon, as clearly as I did yesterday. In fact I'm starting to hear that damn dog all the fucking time. I'd like to tell that dog to give it a fucking rest already.

Ian says absolutely nothing. I assume he can't hear it at all. But staring at him now, sitting across the table from me, his eyes locked on the tabletop, I wonder if I can't actually read his mind after all. I think at this moment and perhaps for the first time, I may be able to discern precisely what Ian is thinking, despite his silence, despite the lack of expression on his big-nosed, pasty face.

If I had to guess...

If I had to choose...

If I had to settle on one thing...

Shutter down, I think he must be thinking. *Shutter down.*

His accent makes the *t*'s sound as sharp as knives.

PART THREE

Unleashed

Each member of the family of four takes a turn staring at me, but I ignore them all. Let them stare. Let them judge. Let them wonder. I have already moved once. I will not be vacating the family of four's compartment. I look past them, out the window. The Hungarian countryside is quite green, quite lush, quite gorgeous as we roar through it. In fact it's so sunny and pleasant, I have to wonder if it's not mocking my rather unstable state of mind, but then I don't really care. I don't give a toss, as they say. The British that is. Oh let's face it, as Ian would say.

There was a terrible scene at the train station. Terrible though quiet. Terrible *because* so quiet.

Radiohead's *Amnesiac* is surging through my Discman. Oh the misery. Oh the pain. Oh the self-loathing. This is totally my kind of music. My hands are drumming my packsack and the half-empty bottle of ice tea hanging off the front of it. The family of four continues to take turns staring at me. The mother glares her disapproval as she catches each of them, but she too gives a curious glance in my direction every few minutes.

What do they see?

My eyes glaze over.

I am thirty.

My name is Anna Woods and I am hurtling through the Hungarian countryside on an Intercity Express bound for Vienna, Austria, bound for Jack, maybe love of my life, maybe mistake of my life, maybe just wants to be friends of my life. Though He says, or rather He writes that He may have always loved me, that I may be *the one*. And though these statements are heady and flattering, it must be noted that they do lack a certain definitive quality, that their most definitive quality lies in the qualifier: may. May changes everything.

You are the one, He could have written. I have always loved you, He could have written. But He did not. He most certainly did not.

And then there's Ian. Or should I say Daddy. What is he doing right now, I wonder. Is he roaming the streets of Budapest? Is he already at a beer garden, and if so, is he celebrating or commiserating? Is he back at his flat, staring out of his ridiculously large and open-shuttered window or maybe lying on his back, staring up at the high high ceilings? Or is he hammering a squash ball? Or is he eating cake? Or is he consulting a lawyer?

There was quite a scene back at the train station (or so I like to imagine), even though it was quiet and nobody probably even noticed us.

Thom Yorke is spinning plates in my ears. I close my eyes and weave my head, drum my fingers on my packsack. I love this song. This entire album is now essential to my survival.

With my eyes closed, I can feel the family of four stealing longer glances. But I don't care. I don't give a toss, as they say. As Ian says.

What no one seems to realise/realize is that I don't have any dignity to maintain.

Ian silently accompanied me on the subway to Deli pu station. He carried the two smaller of my three packsacks. You can see that, even though I am a horrible and perhaps mentally unhinged person, Ian is, once again, a stellar human being, an undeniably good human being, maybe made even more so by his proximity to someone such as myself.

Our final evening together was spent contemplating—though not speaking of—my imminent departure. Perhaps to fill the silence, we engaged in a final screw/shag. Surprisingly it took place in his window frame, that unconscionably large window, and the most amazing part is that he left the shutter open. The shutter was wide open. The sun was setting. The sky was pink.

I pretended it was no big deal, but I couldn't help but think—especially after an old woman down the street came onto her balcony to check the status of her drying laundry—I couldn't stop thinking that we maybe ought to close it after all. (The Frenchman in my head cries: *Puritan!*) Did Ian wish for us to be seen or did he wish to see or was he trying to show me something? I have, I'm afraid, absolutely no idea. The sun never sets on the British Empire, I remember thinking. Stupidly, because there it was: setting.

Still, he needn't have come to the train station with me. Though it occurs to me now that he may have simply wanted to be certain that I left town. And who could blame him really?

I walked precariously under the weight of my big backpack. I am travelling/traveling with a ridiculous number of personal effects. Somehow I seem to have accumulated a shitload of stuff here in Budapest. I get heavier and heavier. We walked down the middle of the platform slowly, despite the fact that the train was idling and due to depart in just a few minutes. I found the car that held my reservation. I stopped. He took two more steps.

"Ian," I said.

He turned to me then. He smiled wanly. There was something in his eyes (I still don't know what color/colour they are) that made me wonder if perhaps he never cared for me at all. Or so I tell myself now. Did he or didn't he? I'm afraid I can't be sure.

"I'm sorry," I said for the hundredth time. Though I still wasn't sure whether he was pissed off or pleased to see me go.

People were pressing past us. Someone handed me a flyer for a hostel in Vienna. Ian said nothing. I couldn't help but think we'd veered from the script somehow. Or maybe even lost it altogether. Weren't train farewells supposed to be full of urgent romance: tearful kisses, passionate I-love-you's, desperate I'll-miss-you's?

I reached out my arms and pulled him into an awkward and limp backpack-laden hug. The flyer was still in my hand. "I'm so sorry," I said again, hoping that he might tell me it was okay or that he would miss me or even whether or not he gave a damn. I heard him smile beside my ear.

He dropped my rucksacks at my feet. "I liked you Anna," he whispered. "A lot."

I pulled back to look at him, but he was already turned away, walking slowly away from me down the length of the platform.

"Ian!" I called, but he kept on walking.

The train sighed. I picked up my bags and clumsily boarded it.

Not pleased, I thought. Definitely not pleased.

The first compartment I entered when I boarded this Intercity Express from Budapest to Vienna was, by all rights, my compartment. If you go by reservations that is. Which the young British backpacking couple (what is with all of these Brits?) obviously didn't, since one of them, an admittedly handsome young fellow wearing funky eyewear was sitting in my seat.

Having just left my own British lover (who now uses the past tense when describing any positive feelings towards me) for some unreliable and ludicrously named American asshole (who may or may not love me, may or may not think I'm the one and may or may not show up in Vienna in which direction I'm now headed), I must confess that I was quite out of my mind. Especially once I realized/realised that someone was in my goddamn spot.

There are six seats per compartment and four of these were already occupied: the young British pair faced each other by the window—one of them, as I've mentioned, occupying what by rights was mine—and an older German (it turned out) couple occupied the two places closest to the exit. The two middle seats were all that remained.

I barreled/barrelled past the older couple, ignoring the fact that I'd probably clobbered the woman's prim face with the Puma sneakers that were dangling off the back of my largest backpack, as both of them were wholly unaccommodating in allowing me into their compartment—no knee movement whatsoever. There was a plastic bag full of snacks on one of the remaining two seats. No one made any motion to move it despite the obviousness, the recent dangerousness of me and my three overstuffed bags.

The train lurched into motion.

Dropping the two small rucksacks on the floor, I clumsily removed my big one and rested it on the open seat. I stared up at the racks. The handsome young Brit with the funky eyewear helped me lift it up into the one small space remaining, but half of it hung dangerously in the air, directly above his girlfriend's head I might add. I sat down between the two men, shoved my other bags as far under the seat as they would go and then stared up at my dangling belongings.

"I'm a bit worried my bag's gonna kill you," I said, assuming—quite arrogantly really as no one had yet spoken—that the girl would understand English; she just looked like such a typical English Rose.

The Rose's face took on a look of horror.

I gestured towards the overhead rack. "Do you think I could move this small bag on top of this case?"

There was general embarrassed agreement, though no one apart from me actually spoke.

But when I tried to lift the small bag, the plump older couple, who were wholly unaccommodating when I'd first arrived to find my reserved seat taken, jumped up in a tizzy of disapproval.

"Bottles," the woman said testily. "Bottles in zere."

The man gently lifted the bag, glaring at me in reproach.

"Sorry," I mumbled, already trying to slide his big case to the left.

The man waved his hands frantically, having just passed the small bag of bottles to his wife. He then took hold of his own big case and slid it over gently, almost tenderly. He offered me a contemptuous smile.

"Thanks," I think I mumbled, but I may have only said it in my head. I slipped my backpack fully—and with safety as my first concern, I might add—onto the rack and sat back down.

Everyone stared at the floor in mute embarrassment.

"I hope the person who reserved your seat doesn't come or we'll have no room at all," the young English Rose whispered to her attractive boyfriend.

"That's me," I said.

"Oh!" she exclaimed, though neither of them made any move to offer me my window seat. Nor did I demand it. I am not the sort of person to demand satisfaction. (Because when has that ever worked?)

Once again, everyone looked away from each other. Or perhaps only away from me.

My stomach rolled. I was facing backwards. The bag of snacks on the seat across from me denied me the opportunity to face forward, which was most unfortunate considering that I am prone to motion sickness. Only moments into the journey, I was already feeling—at the very least—unbalanced.

I pulled out my Discman and switched on *Amnesiac,* anxious to think about you-know-who and that-other-guy, anxious to fully brood over Ian's final words to me—"I liked you...a lot"—so tellingly delivered in the past tense, and also to fully discern any further meaning from Jack's correspondence, the one in which He claimed He *may* love me and that I *may* be the one. Though obviously I may not. It goes without saying that I may not. How quickly things change, I thought, sinking into a deep self-pity. How uncertain all of these relationships are.

But I quickly found myself unable to give these matters my full attention. I quickly found myself quite distracted by the handsome young fellow with the funky eyewear—Mr. Rose as I had dubbed him—who had fallen asleep. He appeared to have closed his eyes and fallen dead asleep against the window, my reserved window, not only *not* taking advantage of his proximity to it, but partially obstructing my own view through it, so that I was forced to stare past both his lifeless body and his girlfriend's deliberately turned-away head just to get a glimpse of the mockingly beautiful Hungarian countryside.

I was furious that they would not offer me what was rightfully mine, that I should have to ask for the right just to sit in my own seat, that they would not even appreciate the sacrifice I was silently making, that the whole thing could bother them so little that one of them could be lulled into a peaceful sleep by the gentle, though nauseating (I thought) swaying of the train.

This would not happen in Canada, I thought. This would so never happen in Canada. And I have to admit that I didn't even care that I was thinking (again) like a boorish tourist. I didn't even care that the above statement may in fact have been false. I was too ill to care. I felt quite remarkably and abruptly ill.

I watched the ground we'd already covered race by the window and silently fumed.

The breaking point came when the conductor collected the tickets.

"Supplement," he said in his consonant-burdened Hungarian accent while staring at the Rose's package tickets. "Six hundred fifty, one person."

I turned triumphantly towards the now-troubled young lovers.

"Supplement?" Miss Rose said, all wide-eyed surprise, as her boyfriend began to fumble through his wallet.

"Six hundred fifty," the humourless/humorless and frankly unpleasant-smelling conductor repeated, whilst examining and then stamping my properly purchased ticket which was stapled to my pointless reservation card. "One person."

"I've only got four hundred," the attractive Mr. Rose said. "Is there an ATM on the train?"

The conductor did not understand this. He shook his head.

Everyone stared at one another for a moment.

"What do we do?" the girl asked, and even I had to admit that the tone she used was seductively helpless.

"No money?" the conductor said. "Bankomat. By Coke and chips."

The Roses nodded vigorously. The boy got up. When he was halfway out the compartment door—he too having to step awkwardly over the unflinching knees of the Germans, though he did not at least have three big bags on his person—the girl called after him.

"Get thirteen thousand," she said. "We need thirteen thousand."

But the boy kept going without a pause. Perhaps he was lost in contemplation of a lifetime with such a hopeless mathematics partner.

Her cheeks were a windswept pink and though I was trying to contain my glee at her misfortune, I fear that I was not doing a very good job. The English Rose kept glaring at me. But I could not help her. I had no resources with which to help her, only a few coins hardly worth counting.

I considered demanding my rightful seat, but abandoned the idea. Not so much out of any altruistic impulse, just that it would require too much of an effort. I listened to Radiohead instead. I thought of Ian, Ian's body, that impossibly lean, big-nosed, twenty-nine-inch-waisted body. Now that it was out of reach, it nagged at me. It occurred to me that he may have been a better lover than Jack, which made me doubtful of my current decision. But then it seemed only fair to give Jack a more current test-drive before I began making such ruthless comparisons.

Still, I couldn't help but wonder how much of my feelings for Ian were simply the desire to be with someone, *anyone*. I was terribly lonely, that much is clear. And all of those couples in Budapest, all of those happy people, and me alone—worse than that, me stood up. Twice. Maybe I was just playing couple.

He was just so fucking nice is all. And so knowledgeable. And...influential really. Leading a huge group in cheers for my homeland? Snogging/kissing at

----

every possible occasion? The bridge? The birthday? Just wrong on so many levels. I was quite out of my mind.

Sitting in the compartment built for six but cramped at five, I strained to miss him, but then I got confused. Jack or Ian? Ian or Jack? I couldn't remember which one I truly missed and which one I wanted to miss, and frankly, the potential pregnancy business was making the whole thing seem a tad gauche.

To my right, Miss Rose continued to glare at me, but I could not help her. I'd spent my last seven hundred *forints* on the reservation that would allow me to board the train at the last minute (as I knew I would) and still get a decent seat.

Mr. Rose came back sweating. "There's no bank machine," he panted. "Just a snack bar where you can pay by Visa."

The girl glared at my Discmanned head. In my ears, Thom Yorke was singing something about souls. I casually turned down the volume.

"Oh no," the girl was saying, quite genuinely really. "What do we do?"

"It is for the reservations?" the German man to my left abruptly asked and I realized/realised that they thought I was the one who did not belong here, that I was the one without a reservation for this compartment and so just barreled/barrelled in willy-nilly, and quite rudely really, considering that they were quite full-up at four.

"No, it's a supplement."

"How much you need?" the man asked, ignoring or perhaps not understanding this last bit.

The Roses looked quickly at each other. "Nine hundred *forints*," the boy said.

Despite a censorious glare from his wife, the man dug out his wallet. He handed them a thousand *forint* bill. I did

----

a rough conversion: five dollars Canadian, three dollars U.S., two and a half quid.

"Are you sure?" Miss Rose asked, but it was already done.

"Give me one hundred back," the German said. I did the translation: fifty cents Canadian, thirty cents U.S., 25p.

"Thank you," said Mr. Rose. "Thank you so much."

The German man shrugged and made a phlegmy vowel sound.

Once again the girl glared at me. But I only had a few coins left, not even worth converting, and so could not have helped them even if I'd wanted to. Which I did not, since her admittedly cute boyfriend was in my reserved seat and carrying an improper ticket besides.

My stomach heaved back and forth with the undulating train.

The German man leaned past me to speak to them. "Vere you travel from?"

"England," the English Rose chirped back. "You?"

I was sitting smack-dab in the middle of these four people, yet they were talking past me, around me, *through me*, as though I didn't exist, as though I didn't matter in the grand scheme of things, as though I *wasn't even there,* which maybe I shouldn't have been. Though let me remind you, I was the only one with a proper reservation.

"Ve live in Vienna," the man with the unflinching knees was saying.

They think I'm American, I thought, though surely the Germans will see my Canadian passport at border control. Do I want them to see my Canadian passport, I wondered, recalling the luggage episode in which I somehow came off the fool, though I was wholly (I think) in the right. (Or at least partially.) I *am* fond of hiding behind the American flag when I'm being particularly obtuse...

"But ve are from Munich."

Perhaps it's best if they think I'm an obnoxious American, I thought, thinking this was possible not only because of my earlier arrogant behavior/behaviour but also because I hail from a country which is, apparently, merely an implication.

"We met some Austrians in Amsterdam," Miss Rose was saying in a ludicrously loud voice as though to make up for the language barrier.

This is intolerable, I thought, my stomach reeling. All I want to do is wallow. Why won't these people just let me revel in my insoluble problems?

"They're going to show us where to drink," the girl was saying cheerfully and loudly.

She is an idiot, this girl.

The German couple nodded happily. I cannot stand these people, I thought. I cannot stand everyone talking past me.

"But you vill not see ze opera."

"We will!" the girl replied.

"But ze opera is closed in August."

"Oh no!" the girl gasped.

And then suddenly, unthinkably, unthinkingly, I was standing up and recklessly pulling down my heavy backpack from the rack just as the train lurched dangerously to the right. I almost took out the cute one.

I was thankful that, even if it was just to stare up at me, at least they had all ceased talking. Pastoral Hungary rolled backwards past the outskirts of my vision. I may throw up, I thought through the sudden silence, then decided that this was no time for such indulgences.

Furiously, and perhaps with deliberate clumsiness, I stepped over the four fat and unmoving German knees and stumbled out into the corridor. I turned round and shut the compartment door on them. I took a deep breath. I moved quickly down the narrow aisle to avoid hearing the aftermath of my exit.

Still, I could not help but note the shrill laughter of the young English Rose just before I slid open the door to the next car. I stood between the two cars for just a moment, gasping at the fresh air, rocking frantically and loudly and now forwardly along with the hurtling train. My stomach churned. When the sound of her laughter began to fade, I pushed open the connecting door and stepped forward.

The family of four smiled warily up at me. I smiled back.

I gently opened their compartment door (apparently having learned my lesson) and pointed at one of the unoccupied seats.

The mother nodded.

Not even bothering with the overhead luggage racks, I parked my large backpack on a seat and plopped onto the remaining forward-facing one with a weary sigh. I extricated my Discman from a zippered pocket, pulled the headphones over my ears, and after a glance at the upcoming scenery and a benevolent smile for the family of four, I pressed Play and sank into a deep and overdue wallow.

The music almost drowned out the shrill resonance of the English Rose's laughter.

Despite myself, despite the shame and uncertainty I feel regarding my decision to leave both Ian and Budapest behind, I am excited. I have to admit that I'm excited. Now that I face forward, there is a gentle and only slightly unsettled warmth in my belly, an awareness of my skin, because in just a few days, I'm going to meet Jack again *after all these years*. Or perhaps the excitement is simply

due to the drama—the misery, the pain, the self-loathing—
that is currently my life.

Whatever. I am exhilarated.

Though I try to quench it. Don't think I don't try to
smother it for all it's worth.

He may stand you up again. Be careful. Be very careful.

But it's far too late for care. Everything has shifted well
past cautious. Just consider the fact that I'm a thirty-year-
old pregnant Canadian woman hurtling through the
Hungarian countryside on an Intercity Express bound for
Vienna. That I have left behind a perfectly satisfactory
(some might say exemplary) British lover for some
unreliable American dipshit (some might say asshole)
named Jack Hammer.

Clearly it is far too late for care. Or caution. Or even a
smidgen of dignity. Yes, I am well past any hope I might
once have held for dignity.

Still, I find myself grinning foolishly as the train
lumbers along on its rails. There is a sense that things
cannot get worse, that some sort of low point has been
attained. And so I am relieved. Except when the nausea
flares up again, at which point I find myself praying
for relief.

The family of four gets off in Gyor. They are replaced by
two middle-aged men who look to be from India or
Pakistan or maybe even Iran. I cannot identify nationality.
I am quite hopeless at discerning race. Perhaps this too is
a Canadian trait, I think. Multicultural mosaic and all
that. But I admit, I am forced to admit that it may have
nothing to do with Canada at all, that it may just be my
own uncultured ignorance. These two men smile cautiously
at me. I manage a pained grimace as reply. My excitement
has vanished. I am now feeling thoroughly nauseated.

Amnesiac is playing again. Still. It has played through
and now started back at the beginning. I am back at the
beginning and sweating profusely. The air-conditioning in

this compartment seems to be quite broken, quite on the fritz, though it is still preferable to my original seat, that sickening, backwards-facing, in-between seat. The August sun blazes pitilessly through the TV-like window. My eyes gaze through the glass but see nothing, trapped as I am inside my uncertain thoughts which go something like this: What makes me think it will be different with Him? What makes me think He is the one?

The two East Indian or Pakistani or Persian men sit motionlessly and silently beside me. I am pleased with these two new neighbors/neighbours. They are so little bother.

I close my eyes and tap my hands. Just because I am on my way to Vienna does not mean I *have* to see Jack, does it? I've got two days. Two days to think. Isn't that what I told Ian I would be doing?

Ian. Jack. Ian. Jack. Ia-

I do not know what I am doing.

And I am so afraid. I am so very frightened, because I cannot help but wonder if neither of them is *the one*? What if neither of them is the one and now I'm not only alone but pregnant too? But then how can I be pregnant? I really don't think I am. I'm sure my period will appear any day now. My stomach somersaults recklessly as though in agreement.

A tall man on a spindly grey/gray bicycle enters the frame of the window. He is rolling down a gravel road that winds alongside a stream. He is old, or the sight of him on his rickety bicycle is somehow old. I get the sense that he's been riding down this same path at the same time each and every day for the past half century. I get the sense that he is a long held tradition, some significant and essential component to the Hungarian way of life, one which I will never be able to comprehend.

Combined with the train's opposite motion, he briefly appears to be hovering over the path. And for a moment, with the concurrence of opposing directions, it is difficult to say whether it is he or I that is actually moving. Or whether we are in fact both staying still.

And then he abruptly disappears from view as the train veers sharply west.

The door to the compartment slams open.

"Passaport," booms a small man with a large gun.

I slip my headphones off. All three of us fumble nervously through our pockets. I find mine first. The man with the gun gives it a disdainful look, then stamps it quickly and passes it back.

He stares at my two compartment-mates. He taps his foot impatiently. Finally the two men pass him dark blue passports. I recognize/recognise these passports. These are Canadian passports.

I smile. I hold up my own official document. They smile back at me. They nod.

The man with the gun stamps twice and then leaves.

One of my neighbours/neighbors opens a plastic bag and peers into it. His friend points at his chest and says, carefully and with great effort: "New...to...Canada."

I nod. I smile.

The other man is now holding out an unidentifiable lump of food towards me. He lifts, then lowers the plastic-wrapped, sandwich-type lump at me again. "You want?" he says in a thick accent, which could officially be classified as Canadian.

I stare from him to the sandwich to him again. How do I ask if it's vegetarian? What fresh hell would that attempt at communication bring? And can I even stomach food, never mind unidentifiable food, feeling quite nauseated not only by my current life and the motion of this train, but also by my seemingly obvious and perhaps even confirmed, yet somehow still unbelievable pregnant state—am I pregnant?

But too much time has gone by while these questions raged through my mind. The man is staring at me suspiciously.

"Thanks," I say quickly. I take the food and unwrap it, though this does not help in the identification process.

I take a bite.

The two men of unknown descent (though presumably they know) watch me expectantly. It tastes like chickpea and...something. It is delicious.

I smile.

The two men smile back at me happily.

We are all Canadian, I think. These are my fellow Canadians.

The hollowness in my stomach fades. I finish the lump quickly, greedily. I was terribly hungry. Hunger was probably at least partially to blame for my earlier motion sickness.

As we cross the border from Hungary into Austria, the two men offer me a pleasant nod and then gaze through the window.

I stare at their snack bag and note that everyone on this train seems to be well-prepared for their journey, whereas I am a snackless mess. I am still hungry and can't help but wonder if my new friends might possibly have another nibble for a fellow countrywoman, but I cannot seem to catch their eye again. I glance from them to their bag of snacks and back again until finally the train slows and begins to bustle with activity.

Vienna appears through the window.

The two men leave the compartment swiftly and without offering me any more of their food.

It is when I am on the platform, fumbling through my pack for that hostel flyer that I see the reservation-ignoring

----

Roses again. Luckily my back is to them and they walk past me before I even notice them. But as I do, Miss Rose turns back to me with what I assume is her version of a sneer. (Though she is far too cute and innocent to pull off such a facial expression.)

She gives an over-the-top wave. "Hal-lo!" she calls out shrilly and pointedly.

I reply with a genuine sneer (I am neither too cute nor too innocent) and then realize/realise at the exact same moment that the hostel flyer is in the smallest of my three rucksacks and that I now have only two bags with me, instead of the original three. I look up at the empty train and try to remember where my place was, where my places were.

"Fuck," I say.

Miss Rose turns away with a triumphant smile.

Thankfully the man at the Lost-and-Found counter speaks English. "You vill try back every few days," he says, though it must be noted that he doesn't look terribly hopeful about my chances.

I understand though. It's okay. This isn't the first thing I've lost. This isn't the first thing I've tried to find. "I'll try back," I say brightly, despite the fact that the majority of my hair products were contained in that bag.

The man nods and looks right past me. "Vel-come to Vien," he mutters.

I instantly collapse onto the single, student dorm/hostel bed that I found listed in the Westbahnhof tourist office. (Oh the humiliation. My name is Anna Woods. I am thirty. I am living in a student dormitory.) My stomach lurches from side to side in reminiscence of the persistent motion

----

of the train. I plant one foot on the floor and begin to pull and pull and pull my fingers through my hair. With every stroke, a strand or two disconnects from my head. I scrutinize/scrutinise each of these loose hairs for split ends. It seems important to evaluate the damage, especially now that my much-coveted protein treatment is lost. (Although it is also possible that I am just helplessly compelled.) Almost every hair is split or splitting or just about to split. It's not just the roots that are the problem. Dead bits come off in my hands. I come to the conclusion—the fairly obvious conclusion—that the entirety of my hair is rotten. And hopeless. And naturally thin—the only thing that's natural about it by the way. And this compulsive pulling is thinning it even further, creating so many layers, it's now practically a shag.

My hair is snapping right off of my head!

I close my eyes. This was not the look I was hoping for. This was definitely not part of the plan.

My stomach sways from side to side. I slow down my breathing and concentrate hard on not concentrating too hard on falling asleep. When I finally sink into unconsciousness, I hear my ends splitting even in my dreams.

Ra-ttttt-ttttt-ttttt-ttttt-ttttt-ttttt-ttttt-ttttt-ttttt-ttttt-(pause)- ra-ttttt-ttttt-ttttt-ttttt-ttttt-ttttt-ttttt-ttttt-(pause)-ra-ttttt-ttttt- ttttt-ttttt...

I wake up Monday morning to the sound of a jackhammer just outside of my student dorm/hostel window. I could be anywhere, I think, wondering where I am. Construction is universal—constantly building up and tearing down, building up and tearing down. The world over. (I do not know what this expression means exactly.)

Shuffling over to the window, I light a Philip Morris *Super* Light.

(Or rather, it's not that I don't know *what* it means, but that its meaning seems so obvious that I assume there must be some more impressive and convoluted explanation behind it.)

Ra-ttttt-ttttt-ttttt-ttttt-ttttt-ttttt-ttttt-ttttt-ttttt-ttttt-(pause)-ra-ttttt-ttttt-ttttt-ttttt-ttttt-ttttt-ttttt-ttttt-(pause)-ra-ttttt-ttttt-ttttt-ttttt...

I crane my neck out of the window and see a jackhammer-mobile. I do not know the proper name for such a vehicle, but it is small like a forklift and the front end holds a jackhammer. A small man wearing a pristine grey/gray jumpsuit sits behind the controls. I watch as he makes the rigid chisel go up and down, up and down, up and down, but so fast that it appears to be in both places at once—up as well as down. It's only the sound that reminds you there's any movement at all.

Ra-ttttt-ttttt-ttttt-ttttt-ttttt-ttttt-ttttt-ttttt-ttttt-ttttt-(pause)-ra-ttttt-ttttt-ttttt-ttttt-ttttt-ttttt-ttttt-ttttt-(pause)-ra-ttttt-ttttt-ttttt-ttttt...

Jack Hammer. As if I need be reminded.

I'm exhausted. I glance back at my travel alarm—7:12 a.m. Typical, these small men and their phallic machines making a ton of fucking racket at completely inappropriate times. (Though I do not, for the record, even believe in women's issues.)

Across the street I can see a neat row of signs and advertisements and posters scattered across a twenty foot long wall. I stare at them wearily as the jackhammer pierces the concrete below. I am amazed to find that I actually understand parts of them—the dates or the location or the artist or one German word that is similar to the English one or maybe even just the gist of the message—but I don't, it seems, I don't understand the entirety of a single one. (Still, this German business already feels a lot more manageable than Hungarian; I haven't understood either a written or spoken word in three months!)

A strand of my split hair wafts through the air in front of me. I make a decision. I suddenly decide something. I must attempt to remedy this hair situation. I *will* do something about this deplorable hair. How can I not take action against this damage?

With a quickly-defeated sizzle, my cigarette drops into the pop can. Smoke billows up briefly from out of the circular tab. I feel irreversibly decisive.

Here I am again, I think just an hour later. About to get my hair done in a city that does not speak the same language as I do, or rather in a city where I do not speak the appropriate language. It's really quite terrifying when you think about it. Some people would revel in it. Ian. Ian would revel in it. Jack would definitely think it a hoot. But not me. I've seen what can happen. I feel only fear, pure loop-de-loop terror.

Because you can gesture with your fingers all you want about how much they should cut off, but what if they think that's how much you want left on your head? Or you can show them a picture, but who's to say they have the skills? Maybe they look at the picture and think *yeah right, that would not suit you sister* and then just proceed to do whatever they want. It's bad enough in your own damn country.

As I walk into the salon, the salon I have chosen (incredibly) from amongst three recommended salons in a just-purchased mini-guidebook and which appears to be the coolest one (though in truth it was the only one I could find), I am armed with a few German phrases taught to me by the girl at the front desk of the student dormitory/hostel I am currently staying in.

I know how to say: *Just a trim.*

I know how to say: *Good.*

I know how to say: *Bad.*

But I do not, it seems, know how to say: *Please help, my hair got fried in Budapest and I do not want to cut it all off but I don't know what else to do and I am meeting the maybe love of my life, maybe mistake of my life, maybe just wants to be friends of my life Jack tomorrow night and I have not seen Him in just years and years and as you can plainly see my hair is horribly horribly fried and I look goddamn Eastern European now and I cannot bear my hair like this, so bad and I simply must have good hair. Especially when I see Him. Especially for Him. I must. What do you think? Is there anything we can do without cutting it all off? Anything at all? Any mutherfucking thing? Please...please help...please help me...*

Unfortunately, the reality of the situation is that I walk in and the receptionist glances up at me and I say *"Sprechen sie Englisch?"* and she shakes her head no and I feel tears well up in my eyes, remembering my last foray into a foreign hair salon, but I mustn't lose it now, so I blink rapidly then make a cutting motion with my fingers which sends the girl into a paroxysm of nodding and I am whisked off into an aqua-green barber's chair where a man with a comb in his left hand and ridiculously sharp scissors in his right looms over me and I don't have the faintest fucking idea of what either of them are saying, nor what I should, or could, say in reply, and so after a few more moments of frantic gestures and uncomprehending head-nodding, I find myself shrugging and leaning back and giving in and letting go. Let go and let god, as the alcoholics say, and perhaps this applies to the entirety of life—though I really would not be the one to say.

I smile at the person behind me, point at my roots and then at his scissors.

The man smiles back at me. He brings me a color/colour sample book.

I shrug sheepishly.

He looks from my hair to the book, the book to my hair. He gives several brisk nods and walks away.

The hour I have spent wandering around Vienna's Ring has impressed upon me a sense of scrupulous maintenance: well-manicured parks, spotless cobblestone streets, even the horseshit from the old-style carriages is almost instantly swept up by street cleaners. Vienna seems to ooze civilization/civilisation. Surely this Austrian man can handle something so simple as my ruined hair.

I open my new mini-guidebook—which I have just purchased at an outrageously jacked-up tourist price—and scan for local attractions. But the words seem to sway back and forth across the page.

The man returns with a pearly white mixture in a plastic dish. He gently divides my hair into sections. I watch without really paying attention.

Am I really going to sleep with Jack, I wonder. Sleep with Him when I may be carrying another man's goddamn baby inside of me? (Although how likely can this be? No really, I'm asking.) Is that really what I'm going to do? Can I be knocked up by one man and bring a totally separate man back to my student dormitory/hostel at the age of thirty for a those-were-the-days shag?

Is that really the plan?

Some stranger, some man with fairly sketchy hair of his own, some guy who doesn't even speak my language never mind show me his references, some strange Austrian dude is dyeing my fried and fucked-up hair in such a blasé manner that it is obvious, it is startlingly clear, that he just does not understand the importance, the gravity, the severity of this hair situation—as though I'm just another head of hair.

Which maybe I am.

Or maybe he just has the situation under control.

Without a common language it's anyone's guess.

I re-open my guidebook and stare at maps of circular streets. I read about the opera and Freud and *apfelstrudel.* I see pictures of the (apparently) famous original *Sacher Torte.* I do not see what is happening to my hair. I refuse to look at what is happening with my hair. Even when the colour/color is washed out and the scissors are unsheathed and large, split chunks of blonde begin to slither down my smooth hair-salon dressing gown in a jovial rush, I cannot look.

In just half an hour, I will walk out of this salon with an overly blow-dried, really-fucking-short hairdo complete with outdated bangs. And the worst part is that my ends will still be slightly frazzled.

On the way to the Lost-and-Found counter at Westbahnhof, I catch glimpses of myself in the shop windows I pass. Well actually I search for my reflection quite purposefully, but still, I am shocked—*shocked*—by the state of my affairs. My roots are...well lighter than they were, and my split ends are mostly gone, but this short hair is quite—*quite*—unflattering.

This is a terrible business, this hair business. There is no way that Jack will want me once He sees this situation. No way at all. Ian never minded my hair, I recall. He thought my fried and frazzled hair was gorgeous.

But then maybe that's the problem. Maybe he should have minded more than he did.

While standing in the middle of a long line for the Lost-and-Found, waiting to check on my misplaced pack, it occurs to me that Ian and I wouldn't have got together at all if it hadn't been for Jack standing me up. (Again.) We'd never have bloody well met if I hadn't been repulsed by the

Londoner. And I would never have even *flown* to Budapest, Hungary if it wasn't for that asshole Jack Hammer.

It is obvious that Ian and I were not meant to be, that Ian and I were not in the cards, that we never should have met at all and that me being pregnant is just an unacceptable concept. Meeting Jack here in Vienna is absolutely the correct decision, perhaps the only decision I could have made.

(All of this decisiveness is so comforting.)

There are an incredible number of people in this line. I am somehow relieved that I am not the only person in this line. Lost-and-Found, I think. How fascinating and odd that these two concepts—so diametrically opposed—actually go hand-in-hand, actually *work* together.

The man in front of me turns around and says something in German.

"I don't understand," I reply.

He stares at me a moment. He gestures at the line-up. "Un-be-lieve-a-ble," he says carefully.

I nod my head. I agree.

The woman behind the Lost-and-Found counter smiles encouragingly. She gets up from her chair and moves out of my sight. The interminable line behind me shuffles impatiently.

How exciting that my bag has actually been found, I think, picturing my travel-sized conditioner and shampoo and my vat of protein treatment and my shine drops and my...

But then a moment later, the Lost-and-Found lady comes back with a strange gloat on her face. She says something in German. She shrugs falsely. Her eyes sparkle.

Schadenfreude, I think, then smile encouragingly so as to lessen her pleasure. I move aside. The person behind me shuffles forward.

What the hell, hardly have any hair left anyway.

I stop at the Westbahnhof *konfitorei* for a pastry treat before I leave the station. There is another long line ahead of me and presently, behind me as well. Everyone is carrying a backpack or a large bag except me. Everyone is going somewhere or coming from somewhere except me. Peering past heads and shoulders, I try to glimpse the upcoming pastry display, but it is quite impossible. I settle in for a long wait.

The crowd is loud. There are half a dozen languages being spoken passionately around me. The noise is not decipherable. I tune it out. I notice a group of five young men in front of me. They all carry colossal backpacks. They all wear khaki, pocketed shorts and Teva sandals. They are large and only nominally less loud than they would be if they were American, but they are so obviously Canadian.

I tune back in. I hear English.

"So what's a *schilling* worth anyway?" one of them says, staring down at a handful of change.

"Ten times more than the dollar."

"Surprise, surprise."

They all moan. They all yuk-yuk. They all wear baseball hats. They look healthy and bright-eyed and good-natured. Polite, but bumbling. They do everything together and in the same way. They blend in. One of them is wearing a Montreal Canadiens t-shirt. These boys are so obviously Canadian, I think, knowing this also, I admit, because of the variety of maple leafs sewn onto their packs.

My fellow Canadians.

Should I say hello? Shouldn't I say hello?

The line moves forward slightly.

"Can't wait to check out some Austrian beer," one of them says.

"Fuckin' A."

These men are yokels. Canadians are so fucking hokey, I think, and at the same time I am amazed at how clearly I can see them now. The one with his cap on backwards—obviously the wild man of the bunch—catches me watching them.

Quickly, I look away. I do not want to talk to these people. I do not want to be identified by these people. What would I possibly say to these men? What could we possibly have in common? Staring at the ground, I wait until the young man turns away and then I sneak out of the pastry shop without another glance.

I walk back to my student dormitory/hostel via a lovely boardwalk by the Danube canal and find myself surrounded by all manner of joggers and cyclists and the occasional roller-blader: Austrians relentlessly and scrupulously maintaining their bodies in the same way that their city is relentlessly and scrupulously maintained. (Will these generalizations/generalisations never cease?)

It occurs to me that I never used to be able to point out a Canadian. Even Ian was better at spotting them than I was.

"Canadians," he once said as we sipped Dreher on Liszt Ferenc ter in Budapest.

I turned to the group walking by. I'd have guessed they were locals except for the Canadian flags sewn onto their packs.

"Why do you do that?" Ian asked. "That flag business?"

"I don't."

"Why do they then?"

I shrugged. "No self-respecting Canadian wants to be mistaken for an American."

Ian sipped his beer. We watched them pass. We could hear a vehement pianist in the Music Academy on the corner.

"Would that be so terrible?" Ian finally asked.

"Ye-eah!" I half-yelled. But then I couldn't help but think it was a good question. "Well maybe...I don't know...I...It's all we've got."

Ian nodded. As though he understood.

Once back in my student dorm room, ravaging a bag of chips from the vending machine, I remember that I need to choose a place for us to meet. I must e-mail Jack with a rendezvous point.

I chew nervously.

Over and over and over again, I imagine the meeting. I wonder how it will really unfold. Will I be hostile or will I be confused? What else might I be? Do I have any other emotions besides these two?

But the whole concept seems ethereal at best: me and this dimly recalled man-from-my-past hovering uncertainly on some empty sound stage.

Oh my god, I imagine I will say. That will be the first thing. Oh my god.

But after that it is only a blank.

I scan my mini-guidebook map: gorgeous building... gorgeous building...gorgeous building...giant black Ferris wheel...gor-giant black Ferris wheel?

Ha!

We'll meet at the amusement park. That seems rather apropos, no? Maybe even *parfait*.

(Ahh, the Frenchman.)

I grab another handful of chips and hurry down to the lobby.

Fear engulfs me.

Having just checked my bank balance on the communal computer of my student dormitory/hostel, I am now convinced, with the same certainty and intensity that I was convinced my ceiling would collapse in Budapest, that someone, *anyone*, can now access my financial accounts. My mind summons up all the backpackers I've seen traipsing through the lobby, passing me on the stairs—a decidedly seedy and untrustworthy lot.

The system used Netscape Navigator. I am used to Internet Explorer where you can Delete Temporary Files. This is a great feature, this Delete Temporary Files. But this option does not seem to exist on Netscape Navigator, or at least I could not find it, though I searched and searched and searched, nurturing a sick sweat in my belly.

Finally, with only a few minutes of my half-hour left, I logged on to my Yahoo! account where not surprisingly, there was no e-mail from either Jack or Ian.

The bottom of the big Ferris wheel, I hastily wrote to Jack. *Riesenrad. Prater. Seven pm. Tuesday. See you there. Anna.*

I wrote nothing to Ian.

And now, walking away from the terminal in an anxious sweat, I am convinced that someone will go on-line and get my credit card numbers etcetera etcetera etcetera and wreak havoc with my past-life, sold-condo finances. Such as they are.

I climb the stairs to my room slowly. I sit rigidly in my student dormitory/hostel chair and stare out my shutterless student dormitory/hostel window gripped by a terrible bout of paralytic anxiety. But I fear it may have nothing to do with bank balances or credit card numbers. One more sleep, I think. After all these years, just one more sleep.

Am I making a terrible mistake? Am I really carrying Ian's baby? I pray I'm not. And the next minute I think maybe it wouldn't be so bad. And the next I vow to quit smoking just in case. And the next I light up a Philip Morris *Super* Light.

Why must this anxiety follow me everywhere and just where the hell is my period anyway? Could that test really have been accurate?

I review all of my files. I gaze blankly out of my window at the neat street below. The jackhammer-mobile is silent and stationary and unmanned. I think: delete, delete, delete. But I can't seem to find the right key combination. I don't seem to even *have* those keys.

Ian. I never felt this anxiety when I was with Ian. I never did. Ian is the good one in this scenario. Ian has done nothing so horrible, nothing so despicable as to stand me up twice in a foreign goddamn city, nothing unconscionable at all. It seems obvious I ought to go back to him.

Course he did lie to me.

But still, he's better than Jack. He's better than...the Londoner. Certainly better than those yokels in the pastry shop. We must stop with this sewing on of our flag business. If we don't want to be thought of as American, why don't we just tell people for god's sake? Why don't we just say it?

We could say: "Hey, I'm a Canadian, eh."

We could say: "Hey, I am not American."

We could say: "Hey, I am not implied."

But then, perhaps the bigger question is why we have to say anything at all.

I am suddenly sickened by my dinner of Austrian potato chips. I fling myself onto my single bed, keep one foot dangling on the floor. With a glance around my room, I try to imagine bringing Jack back here. I was in a student dorm when we were first hanging out all those years ago. Apropos, I think and once again the Frenchman flashes across my mind. (A man for every occasion.)

Yet I cannot imagine anything less probable than bringing Jack back to this room. I do imagine however that I will be fairly hostile when I see Him. Yes, yes I think quite honestly that the strongest emotion I feel for Jack is hostility. Surely this meeting will be a complete and utter disaster.

My stomach tightens. There is an intensity to this anxiety that is unprecedented. I lie in bed. Smoking. Miraculously I doze a little and do not set myself nor the bed on fire. When I awake, my room smells distinctly like a glass washed in dirty dishwater, and there is an abnormal amount of traffic outside of my window—cars rushing past, their headlights veering quickly through my window. Tires squeal. Surely it is these tires that have woken me.

It is Monday night. Why is there so much traffic on a Monday night?

Wide awake, I pull out my Discman and turn on the radio to drown out the noise. I spin the dial. I catch the last half of what must be the new Cake single. Presently the news comes on. The news is in English. I am one hundred per cent filled with delight as I have not heard the news in months. I turn up the volume and immediately learn that there is a Czech nuclear plant which has reopened despite odd vibrations. Some neighboring/neighbouring countries want this plant closed and are now 'monitoring the situation closely,' though the Czech government insists that 'all is well.' All of these countries are so jammed together, I think. It's like they have to care about each other, to some extent.

My forehead creases. Are people fleeing the city? Is that what all the commotion is about? I slip the headphones off to listen again for the high (I think) volume of traffic outside of my window. Has there been a nuclear accident? Incident? Is there some world catastrophe taking place that I—due to language barriers and a perhaps genetic inability to engage with other human beings—am not aware of? I do not miss the news, I think, filling with even more anxiety. As if you would ever hear about a Czech nuclear plant in Canada. And even if you did, as if you would care.

I turn off the Discman. It is best not to know what is going on in the world. It is best to maintain only a vague knowledge of countries outside the pale. Is this why no one pays attention to Canada? Too far away? But then what's America's excuse?

Cars continue to roar by on the street below. Finally I get out of bed and look out the window. Mass exodus does not *appear* to be taking place. No one is fleeing from nearby residences *that I can see.*

I look up. I see stars in the sky and am impressed. There can't have been a nuclear accident if there are stars in the sky, can there? But then just what does a nuclear accident look like exactly? As if I have any idea. As if living in Canada—where nothing ever happens—could prepare you for any such event. (And even if something did happen, we sure as hell wouldn't talk about it. And even if we did happen to talk about it, we definitely wouldn't do anything about it.)

My anxiety intensifies. I turn back to my bed. My room still smells of poorly-washed dishes. I don't know why.

I turn out the light.

I pray for my period.

I close my eyes once again.

I ignore the traffic in the street below.

Tomorrow I will meet Jack. Tomorrow is the day I meet Jack again after all these years.

Can you believe it?

...pregnant...broke...that asshole Jack...short hair...credit card fraud...past-tense Ian...alone...rendezvous point... schillings...forints...exchange rates...twenty-nine-inch waists...Budapest...Austria...Vienna...Hungary... jackhammer...the train...passports...knocked up...thirty...

I must speak to him.

Tuesday morning—the very day I am to meet Jack again *after all these years*—I wake up with an uncontrollable urge to speak to Ian.

I must speak to him.

There was a dream. I had a dream about Ian. It is my first Ian dream and it is so obvious, so transparent— *transparent*—that it makes me cringe.

A bridge is under construction. A huge crane is swinging an entire bridge onto an already planted base. Ian is standing on the base. Of course I am hanging onto the vacillating bridge.

"Jump," he calls. "I'll catch you."

I clutch the bridge in terror as it swings left, then right, then left. It will never slip onto its foundation, I dream-think. Not swaying like this. I am terrified of heights. I am *so* high in the air.

Ian is still calling out to me. His thin arm is stretched out above his twenty-nine-inch waist.

We fucked under this very bridge.

When I wake up, I am still hanging onto the bridge. I have not, perhaps I cannot let go of it.

So transparent!

I am neither sweating, nor breathing hard, nor terrified. I am simply waking from a dream, a terribly obvious and uncomplicated dream. And immediately, before I can even form the actual words in my head, immediately I feel: *I must speak to him.*

(And say what exactly?)

It takes me half the morning to get it all sorted.

I have to find his phone number in Budapest, which I

dimly recall scrawling on a piece of paper with no memorable identifying marks and which turns out (finally) to be lolling between pages 20 and 21 of Tim Parks' *Destiny*, a book I am currently pretending to read—though who can read at a time like this?—drawn to it, I admit, by the title which I am hoping, quite pathetically really, may help to illuminate my current dilemma. Although it also may not. It goes without saying that it may not.

I have to go to the Post Office for a phone card.

I have to find a Post Office.

I have to locate a suitable phone booth, one that is not collecting the heat from the dependable morning sun and at the same time, not too close to the roar of traffic.

I have to figure out how to make an international telephone call from Vienna to Budapest—it takes several tries.

But all of it, all of it I do without thinking beyond the task at hand. I do not, for example, think about the actual conversation I am about to provoke, so that when the foreign buzz suddenly ceases and Ian answers the telephone with his polite but slightly questioning "Hallo...?" I find myself stunned and speechless. My brain stammers. It is still contemplating its recent victory over the Austrian telephone system.

"Hallo...?" he says again into the silence.

I love his accent. *(Say ass.)*

"Hal-lo?"

(Speak already!)

"Hi."

There is a pregnant, so to speak, pause and then finally Ian says: "Oh. Hiya."

I can hear Radiohead blaring in the background. Track four. *Amnesiac.* "How are you?" I ask, fumbling for the right tone.

"Hang on, I can't hear a word you're saying."

Through the receiver comes the sound of his feet crossing the hardwood floor. The music gets quieter. I picture Ian's flat: the ceiling, the window, the brown loveseat, him leaned back in it, me there too, maybe even a crib—can I picture a crib there?

The small screen above the dial pad informs me that I have already consumed ten *schillings*.

"Sorry 'bout that," he says into the phone.

"How are you?"

"All right." There is another lengthy pause. "How are you?"

"I'm...oh Ian," I say, but he says nothing. "I think I've made a big mistake."

Both of us listen for clues in the other's breath.

"What do you mean?" he finally asks. His voice is wary.

I sigh heavily over the difficulty, the impossibility, the strain of this deciding, this engaging. "I mean... you're just..."

"Anna."

It sounds like a warning.

"I don't think I want to meet Jack. I think I...I like you, Ian. A lot. And I think I want to be with you. And I think, if I really am pregnant, that maybe it wouldn't be so bad and is there any chance...?"

He laughs then. It is the laugh he uses when he knows he's not supposed to laugh, that wheezing through his nose. "Oh, that's hilarious," he finally says. "If I really am pregnant. Ha!"

I stare at the glass of the telephone booth.

"Have you gone completely mad?" he says, still wheeze-laughing. "The test was positive darling. Positive. What more proof might you require?"

A smushed-up little car with a *smart* logo tacked onto the hood rolls by the phone booth.

"You think. You don't think. You're never bloody sure..."

"Yeah," I say vaguely.

"What makes you think I want anything to do with you?"

The line crackles menacingly.

What the hell are *smart* cars, I wonder and know at the same moment that Ian could probably tell me. Though god only knows if he would at this point. "I just –" I say. "I want to be with you. Will you think about –"

"I have thought about it," he says quickly. "And I reckon you'd better meet this Jack."

My stomach hits the ground. This deciding business is terrible, humiliating, painful, unnecessary.

The screen above the dial pad says I have twenty *schillings* remaining.

Ian is still talking. "I reckon that until you see this Jack character"—well-earned sneer—"you aren't ever going to be certain who you want to be with and I want you to be perfectly certain you want me."

My stomach bounces back up. "I am sure."

"No," he says. "No, you're not."

"Seriously, I don't care about Jack." I am spurred on by a sudden and profound conviction that Ian is *The One.*

I hear him smile over the phone. "I like you Anna. A lot."

The present tense!

"I like you too." This is like old times. This is so familiar. I feel so light.

"But you ought to meet Jack. Meet him and then ring me back."

Six *schillings* left.

"This is ridiculous," I say quickly. "I don't want to meet Jack. Ian, I want to have your–"

And then the phone dies.

I am frozen, still holding the receiver to my ear, my mouth still pleading.

The dog howls fiercely through my skull. I am sick to fucking death of that dog.

I gently replace the receiver.

Jack is not the only one who led me, I realize/realise. Ian led me through the streets of Budapest for weeks and weeks and weeks. Every night I followed him. Every night.

And it's so obvious now. Of course *He* is the capital. Ian is *Him—The One!*

I am thirty.

My name is Anna Woods and I am totally in love with Ian Wright and I just feel *so light*. I marvel a little at my sudden and profound conviction, marvel at the idea that someone such as myself could have any sort of conviction at all.

I exit the telephone booth with a full-fledged grin on my face and attempt to cross the street just as a car rounds the corner. It is the same car I saw earlier, as though it has circled the block and returned for my benefit. My grin fades as I watch it roll coolly by. The hood reads: *smart.*

Cheeky bugger.

Following in the footsteps of this morning's just-do-it-ness—*I know what I want!*—I am now standing in a very specific phone booth in the main Post Office on Fleishmarkt attempting to make a collect call to Canada, which is not, as I have recently learned, an easy nor a common undertaking for the Austrian telephone network.

They have no operator.

"No operator?" I bellowed to the woman on the street whom I had waylaid for assistance. (Suddenly all this engaging.)

To do so, phone card or no, you pretty much have to come to this one telephone booth in the Main Post Office here on Fleishmarkt and it has taken me all morning to a) figure this out, and b) find the damn place.

Emboldened by my earlier revelation—Ian is *The One*—I have decided to contact my travel insurance company and consult a doctor regarding this potential pregnancy business, which I am determined to deal with whichever way it turns out, dealing obviously being the preferable course of action to not dealing.

"It's been eight weeks since my last period," I say to the insurance operator, still delighted by the message that had asked me to press one for English, two for French; I'd almost forgotten about that. "I don't think I'm pregnant 'cause well I just don't. And I've had safe sex, so I'm worried something else might be wrong."

"Uh-huh," she replies in a Quebecois accent.

Why does she have to sound so skeptical/sceptical? "Is this covered?"

"Blood, urine, x-ray covered," she says tonelessly. "Anything more, you will call us first. Let's see if I will find you a clinic. Hang on."

She puts me on hold.

What was it that I actually saw in Jack, I wonder now. Oh sure we had good sex, great sex even, but let's face it, I was twenty-two: all sex was good.

The connection/connexion to my homeland buzzes static in my ear.

For service in English, press one. Pour le service en francais, appuyer sur le deux.

One please. I'll take one.

Ian, Ian, Ian.

Jack recently wrote that he (no longer a capital) regrets throwing out that silver flask I bought for him so many years ago. Apparently, some time after my twenty-third birthday, after it was supposedly over, both of us systematically removed all items pertaining to the other. Or at least I did, and several years later via e-mail, I learned that he did too. The flask, it turns out, was the first to go.

And he regrets it.

Not that I give a toss what he regrets or doesn't regret any more. But of course not so long ago I did care. Rather deeply really. So the new flask that I bought for him—and that I have already thrown against a cracked Hungarian ceiling—is similar to the old one, but now also engraved.

It says: *To old friends.*

And it must be noted, mostly because this is an occasion for me to detail something fabulous about myself, it must be noted how difficult it is to have English words engraved on anything in Budapest, Hungary. It is not an easy task, not by any stretch of the imagination. But it is done. I have done it.

So now I am standing at the base of this incredibly large and incredibly old Viennese Ferris wheel (which was prominently featured, according to my mini-guidebook, in Orson Welles' *Third Man*, which I am so thankful not to have—how would I handle three?), holding this sappy, engraved gift and wishing with all of my might that I could somehow scrape these letters off. Or at least scratch them a little. But I cannot. And what else am I gonna do with the thing now? Have to give it to the bastard.

(Why couldn't I have lost this stupid flask rather than all of my essential hair products?)

It is 7:05 p.m. and there is no sign of him. Typical. So fucking typical.

A twenty-something dude with light blond dreadlocks and a sunburn is panhandling by the ticket kiosk. The odd thing about him is that he is missing a leg. How does one lose a leg in this day and age?

I sigh and look away, contemplate my Friday appointment with an Austrian gynecologist/gynaecologist, the person who will propel me towards one kind of action or another; I can hardly wait. I re-check my watch—7:06 p.m. Seriously, I am giving Jack five more minutes and then I am outta here.

Mounted in a glass case beside me is a miniature replica of the real Ferris wheel. A placard tells me that the sturdy-looking steel framework, which is sort of riveting in its repetitiveness, dates back to 1897. I cannot help but wonder if its old age makes it more likely or less likely to fall apart.

I check my watch—still 7:06 p.m. Five more minutes and I am ditching this American asshole. And this stupid fucking flask. Though if he doesn't show, who's ditching whom exactly?

My short hair is reflected in the glass case. I stare past myself to the Ferris wheel inside, the framework so strong and confident and unashamed. Shiny too. The red people-shacks are uniformly spaced around the wheel, reminiscent of giant blocks of Lego in both shape and color/colour. Each bears its own number. Each is designed to hold a dozen loose humans, rather than the standard buckled-in couple.

I see the red-and-white wrapping of Jack's gift reflected in the glass as well. It matches the shacks. Why did I have it engraved? Why? Though if all else fails, the one-legged panhandler might like it. I'll give it to him if need be. Maybe a car accident. You could do irreparable damage to a leg in a car accident.

And then I will stick around just long enough to make my Friday appointment, then get myself on the next available train back to Budapest, back to Ian, who is so good for me and so obviously *The One*. I love His accent, His vocabulary, His intonation. Say ass, I'll say, and then I'll kiss Him and kiss Him and kiss Him...

Though I will say the dude looks a tad unkempt. Did the leg get bloody gangrene or some-

"Anna."

The voice comes from behind me. Jack's voice—deep and sexy and slowed-down.

"Oh my god," I say, spinning around one hundred and eighty degrees. "Oh...my...god."

Jack!

It occurs to me that I have not mentioned that time I ran into Jack at a booze-can nine months after my twenty-third birthday and how we talked all night, sitting outside on a concrete parking curb, strangers like shadows surreptitiously arriving and departing, and how it was like old times on that slab of concrete, except that we were gentle and kind and somehow calm and when he finally said, "Come with me," I did, and we flagged down a cab and went back to his place even though we were both attached to other people. And how we had sex, but it wasn't the same. How it was shockingly mechanical and how we lay there silently in the dark, staring at the ceiling, neither of us knowing what to say.

What could we possibly say?

The bed vibrated with betrayal. The bed told me it belonged to some other woman.

As soon as the sun came up I left, wondering—though only of necessity—what I would tell my live-in boyfriend. (I told him the truth, or a version of it anyway.)

I never saw Jack again after that.

And how can I convey what it felt like to hear his voice say my name all these years later without this information, without *all* the information, without all the miniscule details which can never be relayed, which are too intangible for me to ever explain, which I barely even know myself.

How can I explain the quickness with which I forgave Jack for all the despicable things he did to me—the absences, the abandonment, the clap. How can I still forgive him?

I really can't be sure.

Something in his scent maybe. Or just roguish charm. Or the impossibility of him. Or the feeling of him. Or something. He is powerful. Slippery. Maybe more a memory than a man. He grows lighter and lighter as I ruthlessly ponder our every shared encounter and even muse upon those that have been forgotten, are already forgotten, were never remembered, or maybe never even happened at all, until I wonder if the real Jack might not disintegrate like a bit of cigarette ash when you try to pick it up. If he has not already disappeared. If he perhaps never even existed without me at his side. But even I know that this is wishful thinking. I'm just the audience member, the one who gets pulled reluctantly onstage, squirming all the way, but without the power to leave.

Jack.

Just a memory—perverted, fragile from overuse, a cigarette cherry that's been tamped too often and too forcefully, so that it's barely clinging to its base, so that only an experienced smoker can prevent it from falling off completely. Smoking always on my mind.

Jack.

His name. Those letters.

The way they look as I write them—J—A—C—K. Writing them guiltily, hastily, on a slip of spare paper, on a series of nondescript slips of paper, maybe for as long a period as seven years.

Jack.

The way my own handwriting somehow connects me to each letter, to the letters put together, to the person they represent, until the person they represent is maybe less important than the handwriting itself.

Jack.

The way the letters sound when I say them in my head—unequivocal and intimate and almost suffocating. I've always known them. I'll never shake them.

Jack.

Not just a name.

It felt...it felt...*it felt*.

And maybe Ian is no less magic than Jack. Maybe there's just less of Ian inside of me. Maybe there's just fewer letters, fewer scraps of paper, fewer memories to lose.

Jack said: "Anna."

And it was enough. It was enough just to hear him say *my* letters, *my* name. I mean, what more could I want?

There is a woman singing scales somewhere down the hall. Her voice is throaty and operatic and forceful. Though not my usual cup of tea, these scales give me chills. No doubt she is bored out of her skull.

I shiver.

Jack and I are sprawled as best we can across my single-sized student dormitory bed. I hang over the edge, searching for my fags. I light one and exhale slowly, then remember to cough. Jack pays no attention.

"Imagine if that was your life," I say. "Imagine if *singing* was your career. How cool is that?" (These are the types of observational *bons mots* I've had to repress for so many months what with all these language barriers.)

"Ain't very cool if you gotta sing opera."

"Heathen."

Jack smiles, props himself up on one elbow. "Pass me one, wouldya."

I hand him a Philip Morris *Super* Light. "Thought you quit."

He smirks. "I only quit to impress you." He sparks up and exhales loudly. "Like in that movie. Did you ever see..."

Thirty-three now, he still looks twenty-five: smooth skin, *great* skin, his I♥NY tattoo only slightly faded—no sign of any permanent damage from my fingernails all those years ago. He says he's been to the Big Apple now. I guess I believe him. He looks so clean.

I stare into deep, green eyes. I forgot his eyes were green. I forgot what he looked like altogether. He's hot as blazes—I don't even care what he's saying. I nod my head and stare at those long-lashed eyes and I think: Isn't it wonderful that he's talking to me. Isn't it wonderful to look into these fantastic green eyes?

Jack.

When I turned around, when I saw him by the Ferris wheel, I froze. I didn't know what the hell I was supposed to do. He was gorgeous. He *is* gorgeous. I forgot how gorgeous he could be. His lopsided jaw made my knees weak. His hair was shorter, glossier, lankier, his Adam's apple bulging.

He scooped me up into his arms, laughed in my ear. He said: "It is so good to see you again!" He spun me in circles. My legs flew through the air.

I laughed. I cried: "Stop!"

He spun faster.

Dizzy.

He said: "You look fucking great!"

I touched my hair. I said: "Stop."

He stopped spinning. He put my feet on the ground. His smile leaned to one side as he looked over my shoulder and said: "C'mon."

We walked hand in hand past the one-legged panhandler. Jack bought us two tickets for the Ferris wheel.

"I'm not crazy about heights," I whispered.

"It'll be fun. Don't worry."

We walked around the side of the kiosk to the line. We watched as a dozen people were loaded into one of the red shacks. The wheel spun a quarter turn, stopped to unload tourists on the opposite side of the platform and then opened up for a mismatched batch from our side.

The line shuffled forward.

I looked up. I saw an intricate chrome frame. My hand sweated onto Jack's. I got vertigo.

"Jack," I whispered, as we became the front of the line. "I dunno…"

He squeezed my hand and fumbled in his pocket with the other. The Ferris wheel stopped. A crowd of tourists was hustled out of the shack, then the attendant opened the door on our side. Jack leaned forward to whisper to him. Jack handed him something.

The man nodded. The man had ice-blue eyes. The man let us on, then quickly closed the door.

Behind us, the line grumbled.

I laughed. "Just us?"

"Just us."

The box began to move. Windows lined the walls about two-thirds up from the floor. There was nowhere not to see. The blood drained from my face. I stared out the window as we cleared the lush treetops and green Vienna spread out before us. We lurched to a halt at the 9 o'clock position. We were only halfway up and already *so* high.

Jack sat down on the bench in the middle of the red box. He patted the space beside him. "Siddown," he said, and I did. He put his arm around me, looked in my face and frowned. "You really *don't* like heights."

I shrugged and tried to ignore the pendulous swaying. I thought: If I died right now, if this Lego block plummeted to the ground, the headline would read: 'Canadian Anna Woods, 30, and her American lover, Jack Hammer…'

"Wasn't sure you'd meet me," he was saying. "I'm real sorry I didn't make it to Budapest."

The shack cranked into motion again. I held my breath until we stopped at 12 o'clock. I didn't move. The height we had reached was beyond comprehension. I shut my eyes. My palms sweated more.

"Believe me, I know it's not the type of thing you just forgive…man, would you look at this view?"

I heard him get up and go to one of the windows behind me. The box rocked dangerously. I thought about the day Ian took me on the chair lift. It felt like a thousand years ago, but equally terrifying.

Jack crossed the floor back to me. "I know this is totally crazy," he said from somewhere beneath me. "I know we haven't seen each other in…what's this?"

I opened my eyes. He was kneeling in front of me, staring at the red-and-white wrapped package in my hand. The red ink of the paper was bleeding onto my sweating hand.

He grinned widely. "Is it…?"

"For you," I managed to say.

He returned to the seat beside me and manhandled the ugly red-and-white packaging until it lay defeated on the floor. He looked from the flask to me and then back again. "'To old friends'," he read, then shook it and laughed. "You've even filled it." He unscrewed the top and took a swig. He closed his eyes. "Oh man, Canadian rye. Haven't tasted that in forever."

I took my own swig when he held it out to me, but I almost choked. I quickly handed it back to him.

Jack stared at the flask, then looked away. "To old friends," he said thoughtfully. He turned it over in his hands.

The windows that surrounded us beamed in bright, blue sky.

Sky, sky, sky.

I felt terribly ill again. The shack was heaving in the wind. And the rye…

"Just friends?" he whispered.

He leaned in so close that I couldn't see him. Closing my eyes, I felt his lips hover beside my ear.

"I was hoping..." he said.

The shack ground into motion and we began a backwards descent.

"I've been thinking. Maybe you and I should –"

Should.

This was it. This was what I'd been waiting seven years for: my moment, my due, my J–

But just at that moment my stomach churned violently and I burped. Except it wasn't simply a burp. I threw my guts up all over the floor of the shack.

"Jesus Christ!" Jack bellowed, standing up and away from me. "Je-sus Christ."

I sat with my head between my knees and my eyes clamped shut until our little red house once again reached the starting position.

Neither of us said a word.

When I heard the door open, I looked up. Jack was staring at me, not moving. The attendant said something harsh and cursory, which almost certainly had to be a swear word, though it's all German to me—ha ha.

"I think I might be pregnant," I whispered.

"What?" Jack said.

"I said I think I'm pregnant."

Jack frowned crookedly. Then he said: "Hey man, don't blame me. I just got here."

He got me into an American clinic the next day. The nurses and the doctor attended to me with a profitable hustle. They administered a urine test, a blood test, an ultrasound, a swab, a pelvic exam.

"Not pregnant," the Austrian doctor said.

"Thank god," I gasped.

"You are definitely not pregnant. Stress," he said. "Travel stress."

The man has no idea.

He gave me some funky tablets to induce my period. The whole thing cost seven hundred bucks.

Jack extracted his AmEx from his wallet.

Jack said: "It's on me."

Jack said: "Don't worry about it."

Jack said: "It's the least I can do."

We walked back silently to my student dormitory/hostel. He held my hand. He said nothing when I laid down on the bed, heavier and wearier than I'd ever been. I started to cry. I couldn't say why. He fetched me a roll of toilet paper and sat beside me until I fell asleep.

When I woke up, I heard a woman singing scales somewhere down the hall. I thought: Gimme a high C, sister, 'cause I am *definitely not pregnant.* Then I remembered Jack and thought: no, give *us* a high C!

We lit cigarettes and Jack started to talk about movies that were apparently relevant to our situation.

I felt better than I had in weeks. I nodded my head at Jack and stared into his fantastic green eyes.

I thought: It's not a tallied list of pros and cons.

I thought: It's about as choose-able as the country you're born into.

I thought: It's not a matter of capitals at all—Budapest is the capital of Hungary; Vienna is the capital of Austria; Toronto is not the capital of Canada, but it is the capital of Ontario.

Me?

No. I no longer have any need for capitals.

Jack wants to go back to Toronto. "T.O., man," he says. "Now there's a city I'd like to see again."

Because neither of us has been there in ages.

Because both of us are all too aware that we do not belong in this exhaustively well-maintained and hyper-functional city. No, we definitely do not belong here.

Because Jack's gallery debut was a success and he's got to get back to North America to 'capitalize on his good fortune.'

So we're going back to Canada. Next week. And I'm glad. I keep remembering that train ride and the hair salons and the vertiginous Ferris wheel, and I must say, I must confess, I am quite tired of all of this wandering, this travelling/traveling, this relentless recognition of all that is different, all that is not me. And so by default, all that is me.

Jack and I.

Goddamn crazy.

But it doesn't feel crazy at all. More like a smack in the head. A gorgeous smack in the head.

"You're my Mr. Right Now again," I tell him *after all these years.*

He smiles calmly. "Don't you mean still?"

Do you *feel* that?

Ian.

"I have to go and see someone before we go."

"Three days and you're already sick of me," Jack said, leaning insouciantly against my student dormitory/hostel window frame.

"I promise I won't take seven years."

We'd both smiled.

"You can do whatever you want," Jack said. "You know that."

So now I'm sitting once again on an Intercity Express, but this time I'm headed in the opposite direction: from Vienna back to Budapest, on my way back to Ian so I can explain, so I can say goodbye, so I can say—what exactly? I don't know. But I feel I owe him at least this.

I have the compartment to myself and I'm taking this as a good sign. Suddenly, finally, my feelings are taking precedence over my thoughts, though I must admit, I wouldn't mind a little distracting train conversation on this jaunt.

Ian.

"Going to see the dude you were boning in Budapest?" Jack asked as I packed a small rucksack, the one that wasn't lost.

I raised my brows. "Boning?"

"Boning, screwing, whatever."

I shrugged. "Maybe."

"What for?"

"Dunno. To explain I guess, but don't worry. There's nothing for you to worry about."

"You know I ain't the worrying kind. Course you're wasting your time." He glanced up to make sure I was looking. "Anyone with half a brain can see you're the type's always in bed with one dude or another. I'm sure your pal's figured it out."

I stopped packing. I thought: I ought to defend myself. Here is where I defend myself. But somehow I couldn't think of anything to say. The problem was, I could never figure out what the grounds were for my defense/defence.

All I thought was: *Touché.* Too-fucking-shay.

Being back in Budapest is exhilarating—I know where I am! I walk out of Astoria station with a huge grin on my face. Behind me is Erszebet Bridge. Ahead of me the supermarket where Ian and I bumped into each other. Beside that the street where the dog was hit.

I walk up the sunny side of Rakoczi, smiling at everyone I pass. I buy an ice cream from a candy store along the way. The air is thick and wet. Your lungs take it in with much trepidation.

Once outside of Ian's flat, I realise/realize I still don't know his buzzer code. I cross the street to the vacant lot and look up.

"Ian!"

A dour-looking woman in a nearby building leans out of her window. I smile. She retreats.

After another moment: "Ian!"

"Ian who?" a voice calls from down the street.

I turn to see his twenty-nine-inch waist sauntering towards me. He looks even taller, thinner, pastier than I remember him looking. More British than ever. Compared with Jack. Now that I can really compare him with Jack.

"Nice hair," he says.

I cannot tell if he's 'taking the piss.' I'm still not clear on this 'taking the piss' business. I reach up a hand and flick my bangs just once. "How are you?"

He curves an arm around my waist and leans down to kiss me. I turn my head stiffly, so that his lips land adjacent to my mouth. He stares at me for a long moment, then glances round the street.

"Right then," he says. "Fancy a pint?"

I exhale. "Definitely."

There is a minuscule sidewalk café down the street from Ian's flat. We secure one of the two tables, order a round of

Dreher and lean back mock-comfortably in our cheap plastic chairs.

Ian lifts his glass. "Cheers."

"Right." I laugh nervously. "Cheers."

I can feel my thighs sticking to the seat beneath me. The table is ridiculously close to the street, right at the point where the road bends sharply. We watch the traffic roll by for a while, breathing in strident gusts of exhaust, then I tell him about my recent-and conclusive-exam. He nods expressionlessly. He stares at the table, the roaring cars. Then he tells me about a brand new batch of students. I nod expressionlessly. I stare at the table, the roaring cars.

"...a native speaker says bumped into," he is saying. "A non-native speaker would say met up with. Isn't that interesting?"

I smile indulgently: the 'TESL wanker.'

"It's interesting, isn't it? All the clues you reveal about yourself without even knowing you're doing so. Like you're clearly Canadian, I'm clearly British. And then all the various sub-categories."

"What's Canadian?" I ask, suddenly frantic for him to answer this question for me, suddenly aware that I care about the answer to this question—maybe for the first time. "Tell me what Canadian is."

He smiles at me, exhales slowly and for a moment I can barely see his face through the smoke. "Oh Anna," he says in the voice he must reserve for his students. "You know perfectly well. Quit acting as though you've got no idea."

I smile back at him, take my own slow drag and stare at his dark curly hair, his white skin, his big nose, his oh-so-British face. I recall how soft his lips are, how small his waist is, how smooth his chest is. It occurs to me that I'm not completely averse to a farewell shag/screw. And maybe even that it could just as easily be him. I could just as easily stay here, actually stand Jack up for a change. And stay with Ian. Or Jack. Or Ian. Or Jack. And maybe either is as good as the other.

Which is completely ridiculous. But also, somehow, Canadian. I smile uncertainly at Ian and clutch at my pint.

"Oh my god," I say.

"Wha-at?"

"I think I just figured out what being Canadian means."

Ian frowns, then says: "Jack."

"What?"

"Jack," he says again. "What's he look like?"

"Uhh…"

Ian stares past my head. "Stocky, shrouded in black, tattoo on forearm, poncy blond hair."

I blink rapidly.

"He's watching us from behind that — oh Christ, did you bring him with you?"

"No! I —"

"Oh, there we go," Ian says looking suddenly down at the table. "On his way over. Bloody hell."

My mouth drops open just as I feel a hand on my shoulder. I twist my head. Jack flashes his crooked grin.

"Hey honey." His fingers press down hard on my skin, making me wince. "Aren't you gonna introduce me?"

I turn back to Ian who is nonchalantly sipping his lager, though he is watching us carefully. Hazel, I think. That's the colour/color of Ian's eyes after all. Just hazel. It's so simple, and all this time I was looking for something so much more complicated. I gulp and ignore my fierce blushing.

"Ian, this is Jack. Jack, Ian."

"Jack Hammer," Jack booms, extending a hand. "Good to meetcha, man."

Ian shakes the hand with distaste. "Jack…Hammer," he repeats. "That your real name then?"

- -

"He-ell no. Just a nickname I got stuck with. First name's actually Ball-peen."

Ian and I blink at him. Jack ignores us and drags a chair over from the next table. It makes a harsh, grating sound. He pushes it beside me, which forces Ian to shuffle his seat a little to my right.

"But Jack is actually your name, right?" I ask, amazed that I could be unsure of something so fundamental.

Jack ignores me, sizes up Ian instead. He leans across the table and says, "I hear you were boning Anna just before I got here."

I stop breathing.

Ian smiles calmly. "Don't know if Anna told you, but the service in Hungary is abysmal. I reckon you'll want a pint?"

Jack grins wider. "I *reckon* I will."

"Allow me," Ian says and walks inside with a deadly straight spine. (Definitely taking the piss.)

I turn back to Jack who is leaned back in his chair looking rather pleased with himself. I say: "What the fuck is your problem, Ball-peen?"

Jack points at his chest and raises his brows De Niro-style. "You talkin' to me?" He looks over both shoulders. "I don't see anyone else around here. You talkin' to me?"

"What are you, following me?"

"You think I'm gonna let you just wander off and spend an afternoon boning Iggy Pop here?"

"What happened to freedom, dude?"

"Lemme tell ya somethin', honey. Freedom don't apply to situations like this."

Ian reappears with three fresh pints and a pair of rosy cheeks. "We were just talking about Canada," he says, doling out the amber liquid. "Anna was just about to explain the Canadian mystique. I think she's having a bit of a patriotic fit."

"I'm not having a fit." (Why am I so angry?)

Ian continues as though I'd not spoken. "Any thoughts?"

Jack lifts his glass. "My thoughts are…" He puts a finger on his chin in mock-concentration. "…bottoms up!"

Ian purses his lips. "Cheers."

"Oh, right." Jack rolls his eyes. "Cheers."

"Might want to be careful," Ian says to Jack. "The beer here is likely stronger than you're used to."

"Don't worry, dude. I can handle it, lived in Canada for awhile."

"Did you?"

"Yeah, man. Over a year in *Toronna*. Anna didn't tell you?"

"No. To be perfectly honest, she hardly mentioned you at all."

They both turn to me. I smile sullenly.

"Canada, man," Jack says. "*Quite* an experience."

"Decent beer then?" Ian asks.

"*Totally* decent." Jack takes another swig.

"And?"

Jack frowns. "And what?"

"Well, any further observations?" Ian leans in. "Anna seems to be having a bit of an identity crisis. Maybe you could sort her out."

"Maybe I could sort *you* out."

Ian sniggers.

An ambulance screams around the corner and wails down the street. The three of us are silent until it fades away.

(Am I having an identity crisis?)

Ian leans conspiratorially across the table to address Jack, as though I am no longer present. "To be perfectly honest, I thought she was American at first."

"Wha-at?" I say.

He turns to me reluctantly. There is no discernible expression on his face.

"You seriously thought I was American?"

Ian shrugs.

(Of course I'm having an identity crisis; I'm Canadian. This is what we do. I want to scream something. Something like 'I demand satisfaction for my allegiance!' But…)

"Canada's clean, man," Jack offers, perhaps just catching up. "And the people are so nice."

"Nice and clean," Ian smirks. "Well, that's terribly helpful, now isn't it?"

Jack sighs. "Listen pal, I just dropped by to let you know Anna's with me now, so she won't be needing your…services any more."

Ian makes a face. "Bit odd that she came back to see me then, isn't it?"

"Not really. Our Anna's a nice Canadian gal."

Ian turns to me. "Just came to say goodbye then, did you?"

Jack turns to me as well.

My eyes flick from one to the other. I smile uncertainly, a reflexive effort to please both of these men at once. I have to admit that a large part of me is enjoying this. I have to admit that being the centre/center of attention (finally) is quite intoxicating. Will they come to blows over me? Is this what I've been looking for: to be wanted?

Jack is apparently psychic. "You want me to kick his ass, Anna?"

"Yes, go on, Anna. Should Yankee Doodle Dandy kick my ass?"

Ass!

I can't help but smile. I *love* Ian's accent. I *love* Jack's bravado. Both of them are staring so intently at me that I am reluctant to let the moment go. I look from one to the other, more than a little satisfied. I think: They see me. They want me. They make it seem like I actually get to decide.

"Anna?"

And it's just so painfully clear to me: the Canadian way is precisely this lack of decisive action, this unwillingness, perhaps even refusal to chart a course, to choose to be *one thing and not another*. And so perhaps it's my nationality more than any specific character defect that is to blame for my unceasing irresolution here.

Jack. Ian. Ian. Jack. It could be either one of them. There's a difference, but not really. And more importantly, neither one is as good as the both of them together. And that's just the way it is.

For service in English…

"Hel-lo…Anna?"

I look at them sitting side by side. "I…well…why don't we all *go* somewhere?"

"Wha-at?"

"The three of us," I say. "We could see Romania or Poland. Or Bulgaria. We're close to everything here and it's cheap. We could have a great time."

"Are you quite all right?"

Jack frowns.

"C'mon you guys. I'm serious. It would be fun, don't you think?"

They turn to look at each other and I am suddenly very turned on. This is the answer. Finally an answer I can live with, an answer that *feels* right.

"A right madam you are," Ian finally sniffs.

I look to Jack who is shaking his head.

But just because it feels right does not make it work. Hovering between these two so does not work. I am suddenly repulsed by the both of them, with their *fits* and their *mans*. I look quickly down at my pint. I don't want either of these men. I don't *need* either of these men. Yet here they both are.

"That's not how it works," Jack says softly. "It's either, or. That's just how it is."

"Is it?" I whisper back. "Is it really?"

I am sick to fucking death of these dudes telling me what to do and how it works and the way it is. And surely this is why I am so angry.

An uneasy silence clings to the table. Each of us stares into our separate glasses. I am trying not to emanate the repulsion that I suddenly feel for the both of them. They don't understand me at all. How could they ever understand? With their monarchy and their melancholy pop music, their slick movies and their blind patriotism. Not that I understand them either. In fact it occurs to me that I have no idea who these men really are...

"What's it like?" I say.

They both look up.

"To be so sure."

They frown, confused.

"To know and be known."

They blink at me.

"To actually get satisfaction from your..."

But I cannot finish and strangely, at that exact moment, I finally feel my heart begin to break, the languorous splitting apart I seem to have been expecting from the very moment I arrived here. But it is not splitting for them. Not for either one of them.

I stand up from the table, busting apart from the inside out. I have got to get away from these two, I think. *I have got to get away.*

(But nicely.)

"*Csokolom*," I whisper to Ian who turns to me with a look of confusion spreading across his pasty face. Then I turn to face Jack. "*Csokolom*."

I smile a little as I consciously memorise/memorize the two of them together, sitting side by side as they are. I see them clearly as they stare up at me, then I abruptly turn around before either one can think to look away.

"What the fuck does *that* mean?" Jack asks behind me.

And it's probably because I am listening to Ian's response—"It's Hungarian. It means I kiss your hand."—and also because I hear a peremptory snort from Jack and also because I am concentrating on picking my way through at least one sick dog's scattered excretions that I do not notice the speeding Trebant rounding the corner and heaving towards me until it is way too late to do anything about it.

I look up, frozen.

Someone yells something.

I feel the centre/center of my heart give way with a final tear, fully splitting apart into two separate pieces.

And then a rush of noise and I am gone.

It's red. And concentrated. Almost a glow. Small, but definitely standing out from the haze of beige surrounding it. I try to focus my eyes. Nothing changes. I close them.

The air is thick with foreign voices and smells, a slightly perturbed bustle. I have no idea where I am. I re-open my eyes. Again I see the red glow. I focus and it becomes clear: a red maple leaf. A person is leaning over me and this red leaf seems to be attached to his head, emblazoned across it. Some distance behind the leaf, looming over me from afar are two more familiar figures.

And it all comes roaring back to me.

Ian.

Jack.

Jack.

Ian.

"Are you okay?" the maple leaf calls out to me from his vigil above. (These fucking Canadians are everywhere.) "Are you okay?"

The guy wants to know if I'm okay. And oh how I would laugh if only this terrible pain in my chest would go away.

"I think she's gonna be okay," the voice says.

I seem to be lying on concrete. I wiggle my toes. Seems all right. I do my fingers. S'okay. There is a disturbing smell: beer and dogshit and something metallic.

"Are you all right?" the voice calls out once more overtop of the noise.

And again, I am struck by the urge to laugh. There is an argument in the background. Yelling. Shouting. Accusing. It is happening in a foreign language, but the tone is unmistakable. (Course the Hungarian language always sounds this way to me; my utter lack of comprehension imposes a threatening edge upon it.) And now a voice I can understand jumps in.

"What the fuck is your problem, man? You don't look where you're fucking going?"

Jack.

A man replies in indistinguishable rapid-fire consonants.

"Anna? Anna can you hear me?"

Ian.

Jack, Ian. Ian, Jack. And lying here—flat-out like so much dog-shit though seriously lucky to be alive—it's difficult for me to recall what all the fuss was about. I feel strangely free of all the fuss. Neither of these men is *The One*. The concept of a one, for someone such as myself, suddenly seems about as relevant as the concept of customer service to a Hungarian. I mean it just doesn't apply.

A small crowd has gathered around. Gazing up at them, it strikes me how familiar the Hungarian physiognomy is. It's not just the Americans and the British, I reflect. I can see the whole world in my own country: French and Persian and Dutch and Australian and German and Chinese and Japanese and Greek and Italian and Filipino and Hungarian and Egyptian and Chilean and Polish and Korean and Brazilian and Mexican and South African and all the flags outside of all the hotels of all the world.

I turn away from the familiar faces and glare instead at the maple leaf. Such a brilliant red, the stem so impossibly dainty, the thick middle divided so decisively into three pronged sections, each of those sections divided again into jagged points: a prickly sort of emblem, but one which I have to admit is emitting some kind of sick power. Lying here on this filthy Budapestian pavement, I can definitely feel the power of this leaf. Deep from within me comes a visceral tug, something recognizable/recognisable and innate, something that is undeniably mine, some kind of indefatigable defeat— even here, flat out on my back, nearly dead. And it's probably the suddenly lying down on the pavement that makes me see it: we wear them to find each other, to find our selves.

Ha!

My name is Anna Woods and I am a Canadian through and through.

(It's possible I am slightly delirious.)

I let my eyes lower to the man beneath the emblem. Something about him reminds me of the Londoner. Probably it is his Vancouver Canucks t-shirt. He smiles at me. He is not wholly unattractive. I smile back.

"You took quite a tumble," he says. "Can you move your toes?"

I nod.

"Careful," he says.

"I'm okay," I say, trying to sit up through a rush of dizziness.

"Whoa, whoa, whoa," the kind stranger says. "I think you better lie still for awhile."

I wholeheartedly agree.

"You're lucky I was passing by," the man says. "I saw the car coming, and pushed you out of the way. Prob'ly pushed a bit too hard."

The concern on this man's face is overwhelming. The concern on this man's face is going to make me cry.

"Have you got a cigarette?" I mumble, mostly to change the subject.

He frowns and shakes his head. I can see the 'You-shouldn't-smoke' tape jamming reluctantly behind his eyes. But in the background, reliable Ian is fumbling open a new pack of Philip Morris *Super* Lights. His hand shakes as he leans down and places a fag between my fingers. I stare at it, stare at him, then at Jack who has rejoined the circle of faces above me.

What does this remind me of?

And then I hear it. A sudden raging howl, not vowels or consonants or words—just pain and shock and fear. And I wonder if I might be making this sound. But no. It's the husky, that husky that I saw so long ago, howling like a grievous child right after it was hit by that truck. Or that car. And with stunning near-death perspicacity, I realize that, once again, I'm being an idiot. Who gives a crap *what* hit the dog, the point is that the dog survived the hit.

The dog lived.

The dog howled.

The dog fucking *triumphed.*

That was the dog's message. That's what that fucking dog was trying to tell me: survival is its own bloody victory.

I open my mouth, but no sound comes out, only a bittersweet taste spreading across my tongue. It has an ominous permanence about it. Jack and Ian loom in the background, but seem very far away.

With a fierce conviction, I crush the Phillip Morris *Super* Light against the pavement, relishing the decisive snap of the paper wrapping. I cannot bear this fucking dependency.

(It's entirely possible that I am not all right.)

"I think you're going to be just fine," the maple leaf says at exactly the right moment. "Just need to take it easy for a while. You've had quite a shock."

"You're Canadian," I say.

He blushes slightly and touches his cap. "Yep. You too?"

I nod.

"Heading home today," he says. "Been backpacking around for a few months and just got the urge to haul my ass back home. Never thought I'd miss it."

I struggle to sit up.

Jack and Ian lean in.

One or the other says: "Anna, are you all right?"

I ignore them and lean into the maple leaf who is wrapping an arm around my shoulder for support. The crowd is clearing now. There is no blood, no gore, nothing of interest here. Ian and Jack struggle to get closer now. I see each of them reach out a hand.

"Anna."

"Anna."

One or the other says: "Thank Christ you're all right."

I stare at the outstretched limbs, but I no longer have any desire for them.

The Canadian says: "Think you're ready?"

I nod.

"Easy now," he says, wrapping my arm around his waist. "Nice and slow."

I lean into him as we struggle to our feet, struggle to stand up straight. I close my eyes until the dizziness passes, and then I put my lips to his ear and whisper.

"Take me with you," I say.

And I have never been so sure of myself in all my life.